Dark Kisses

By

Rachel Carrington

Venus Press LLC

DARK KISSES

This is a work of fiction. Names, characters, places, and incidents are either the product of the author's imagination or are used fictitiously. Any resemblance to actual events, places, organizations, or persons, living or dead, is entirely coincidental.

First Printing March 2006
Dark Kisses
Copyright © 2006 by Rachel Dawn Carrington
ISBN: 1-59836-259-3
Cover art and design © 2006 by Sable Grey

For information, you can find us on the web at
www.VenusPress.com
PO Box 584 Hillsborough, NC 27278

Chapter One

The road stretched before him long, dark and desolate. The humming of the engine was the only sound except for the night winds blowing in the opened window.

Ty drove with one hand on the steering wheel, the other resting on the stick shift at his right thigh. Having no desire to listen to the twangy sounds of talk or banjo country, he'd killed the radio about a half hour before as he drew closer to the small town of Peking. Now, he was alone with his thoughts and sometimes, they were louder than any sound a radio could make.

He wondered what he was doing and why he was doing it. He'd been an operative with the CIA for over ten years and he'd slowly climbed the ranks until he was wanted in every section. The CIA knew he could get the job done; he just wondered how he could do the things he did and not care about the people who got hurt along the way. He was an emotionless machine, using his body as a tool to restore justice, catch the criminal and right the wrongs. But he wasn't happy. In fact, he wasn't even sure he'd know happiness if it walked up to him.

His light green eyes drifted down to his forearm and he frowned. The son of a Jamaican man and a Caucasian woman, he was comfortable with his skin, but others weren't. He'd grown up in a large city, which should have made his childhood easier; it hadn't. Bigotry was everywhere and he'd endured a lot of it until he'd shot up to his current height in the seventh grade. Suddenly, the taunts had ceased and everyone wanted to be his friend. His lips curved into a smile. He can't say that he blamed them. To the little guys in seventh grade, over the summer, he'd become a giant. And gained the respect he'd so desperately craved.

The lights of the town winked in the distance and Ty slowed the Porsche to the proper citywide speed limit. It was a straight shot through town to the small hotel on the outskirts. Having reserved a room in advance, Ty had only to show his ID and pick up his key. He was looking forward to a good night's sleep before he began his search the next morning.

The hotel room was simply furnished with a double bed, faux wooden round table with two padded chairs and a long dresser secured to the wall below a same width mirror.

Ty tossed his bag to the bed and out of habit, removed a small, black box and checked the room for any listening devices. Not that anyone in Peking was suspecting him, but he was always on-guard, expecting what others didn't. Perhaps it was what had kept him alive all these years when his fellow colleagues were falling by the wayside.

The air conditioner clicked on with a low whir while Ty removed his shoulder holster and placed it on the dresser. Slowly, methodically, he stripped his shirt and stuffed it into one corner of the duffel bag. The silence was deafening and made him crave the sound of music, the rhythm of a steel guitar, anything to drown out the sound of his own breathing. God spare him from small towns. Leaning forward, he twisted the knobs on the shower and stepped beneath the heated spray.

* * *

The only contact listed in the manila folder was Peking's only attorney, a woman by the name of Caroline Winslow and Ty was standing out in front of her office bright and early the next morning. The only problem was the office was locked securely with a closed sign on the door. Ty checked his watch. Just after nine. What time did lawyer's offices open anyway? He settled back against the brick wall beside the louvered door and decided to wait.

* * *

Carrie left her house at a little after ten, her steps determined. Having been waylaid by her mother yesterday en route to the spa, she had never made it to her relaxing session of mud and steam. Today, however, was a new day and she was going to have that mud bath even if she had to drag her mother along with her and listen to her babble while the mud sank into her pores.

Dressed casually in white pedal pushers and a striped black and white sleeveless sweater, Carrie prayed she didn't run into any member of her family. A long explanation would ensue as to why she wasn't opening the office for the second day in a row. Well, she was determined to forget about them, even if for just one day. She hadn't taken a vacation in four years and she deserved one. In fact, she was long overdue for one.

Sliding behind the wheel of her Mitsubishi 3000GT, she gunned the engine, dropped the gear into reverse and backed out of the driveway of her one-story ranch house, eager to be on her way. She could almost feel the tension ebbing away from her muscles.

* * *

An hour later, Ty was tired of waiting, not to mention irritable and hungry. The continental breakfast the hotel had offered hadn't been what he was accustomed to eating to support his muscular frame. Spotting the overhead sign that directed him toward the only diner in town, he hastened his steps toward the small restaurant.

The bell jangled and all conversation ceased. Diners swiveled on stools and in their chairs to get a better look at this visitor to their town. Men and women alike craned their necks to see his face and then, female eyes covertly slid down the powerful frame clad in tight-fitting blue jeans and an impossibly tight t-shirt that stretched across broad biceps and molded to his impressive chest. But in the end, it was the face that captured their attention once more. Mocha-colored skin, startling hazel eyes, high cheekbones and full, sensuous lips that begged immediate attention riveted eyes and elicited soft sounds of appreciation. It was a face that could only be described as beautiful, classic and surrounded by thick, long braids that fell well below his shoulders, it was a face that demanded awareness.

Sharon removed her apron and approached the visitor. "Hello. I'm Sharon. Come on in and have a seat. Forgive us all for staring. It's just that we don't get many visitors around here nowadays."

Ty moved toward the counter and seated himself upon a red upholstered stool. To his left sat a large man with horn-rimmed glasses and thinning brown hair; to his right, a grandmotherly woman with silver hair scraped back into an unflattering bun and bright blue eyes that didn't bother to hide her interest. He nodded at both and faced forward. "Coffee, please."

Sharon beamed at him. "Certainly. Would you care for some breakfast?"

"That would be good and I'd also like some information, if you can give it to me."

Every ear in the diner strained for the question.

"I'll help if I can." Sharon paused in the process of filling a large, white mug with freshly brewed coffee. "Shoot."

"I'm trying to find Caroline Winslow."

"Well, obviously, you don't know her if you're calling her Caroline. She goes by Carrie. She's our town's lawyer." Sharon slid the cup of liquid caffeine toward him, her smile broadening. "I wish I could help you, but I noticed that she didn't open up shop this morning. She must be taking the day off."

"That's unusual for Carrie," offered a voice from the back.

"Maybe she was just tuckered and needed a rest," came a female voice from the opposite end, a bit defensively, Ty noted.

Ty swung his gaze toward the sound of that voice. "Ma'am, would you know where to find her? I have something very important to discuss with her."

The woman moved forward, slender, perky, with a pretty face and an easy smile. "Well, the way I heard it, she was going to try out the new spa that just opened up a couple of weeks ago."

Ty nodded his appreciation. "Thank you." He tipped his head and tossed back the hot coffee without batting an eye. There were murmurs of surprise when he stood up, tossed a five-dollar bill onto the counter and flashed Sharon a smile that was both powerful and enticing. "I appreciate your help, Ma'am."

Sharon flushed and waved a hand in front of her face. "Aren't you going to have that breakfast?"

"I'll be back. I have to take care of business first." He continued to smile at her. "Thanks again."

"Oh, please. I didn't do much of anything. You just come back when you can stay longer." She was still watching the glass door long after he'd walked out of sight. "My, my, my. Wasn't he a fine-looking specimen."

A snort of disapproval greeted this question. "Doesn't look like he'd fit in here."

"For a man like that, we'd make him fit." Sharon returned to her duties, whistling.

Chapter Two

Carrie pressed her mud-covered face against the thick terry cloth towel, breathing in the fresh scent. Curling her arms behind her head, she stretched out on her back atop the massage table, her toes furling upwards in sheer ecstasy. She couldn't remember the last time she'd been so pampered and she was enjoying every minute of this mini-vacation.

"Ms. Winslow?" The deep voice brought her upright with a start. She whirled around on the table, her slippery skin causing her to slide dangerously close to the edge. Her hands reached out, grasping for a hold, something to keep her in one place.

A strong hand closed around her wrist and hauled her upright, saving her from landing face forward on the carpeted floor. "I apologize for startling you." The voice was laced with amusement and an accent that Carrie couldn't place.

Sitting lotus style, Carrie glared at her visitor. "If you could read, the sign on the door says do not disturb, Mr--" She paused to let him fill in his name.

Ty reached for a nearby towel and handed it to her. "Hamilton. My name is Ty Hamilton and if you wouldn't mind covering up while we continue this conversation, I'm sure we'd both be more comfortable."

Carrie's eyes dropped to her naked breasts and with a low sound of disgust, she yanked the towel from the stranger's hand and tucked it around her slim figure. "Well, I'm sorry if I offended you, Mr. Hamilton, but I wasn't expecting visitors."

"I need to speak with you."

"You are speaking with me...in a very awkward situation, I might add." She continued to glare up at him, taking note that her neck was beginning to ache, but she wasn't about to invite him to have a seat.

"I'd like a more private conversation area, if that would be possible." Ty didn't move, effectively barring any possible exit to the door that she might be contemplating.

Making sure the towel was securely in place, Carrie slid to the floor, pushing the terry cloth down over her toned thighs. "Then I would suggest you make an appointment."

"I went by your office, Ms. Winslow. As you well know, you were closed." Hazel eyes dropped to her vividly colored nail polish before climbing back up silky long legs the color of golden honey before finally reaching her mud-covered face once more. Carrie watched the inspection, feeling her skin warm beneath the intensity of those incredible eyes. Ordinarily, she wasn't one to notice a man's eyes immediately, but these were riveting, capturing her, holding her.

Feeling self-conscious about the mud-pack and her state of undress, Carrie kept her eyes trained somewhere in the vicinity of her visitor's feet. She wondered where his eyes were right now, but she wasn't brave enough to lift her face to look. Determined not to be held by the stranger's compelling presence, she padded toward the sink on bare feet. "Then call tomorrow and my secretary will be more than happy to schedule an appointment for you."

"I'm afraid this can't wait."

"Everything can wait in Peking, Mr. Hamilton. We don't have any emergencies here...unless you count when Mrs. Baker's cat got treed, but that didn't even make the evening news. Now, are we done here? Because I'd really like to wash my face and get dressed. Now that you've interrupted me, I'm feeling inclined to leave."

Ty leaned one shoulder against the closed door. "I know this probably isn't what you want to hear, but I'm afraid I must insist that we talk today."

She bristled at his imperious tone. Okay, so the man did look like a Greek God, but the last time she checked, he was neither her father nor her employer. She didn't answer to him and demands always made her spine stiffen. Injecting a chilly note into her voice, she replied, "And I'm afraid that your insistence means squat to me. I don't know who you are and other than your name, you've given me very little reason to believe that this is a matter of extreme urgency. Now, if you will excuse me, I have other plans and once again, I am asking you to leave."

Ty's hand dipped into the back pocket of tight-fitting jeans and he retrieved his wallet. Carrie was surprised that anything could fit between the snug material. "I'm an undercover operative with the Central Intelligence Agency. I've been sent here to investigate one of your town's citizens. Your name was given to me as the only legal contact in the area. I reiterate, I must insist that we talk today."

Carrie's eyes lingered on the badge before she looked away and pulled in a deep breath. "Well, since you put it that way, meet me at my office in thirty minutes."

One eyebrow arching, he scanned her mud-covered face. "Only thirty minutes?"

Carrie restrained herself from demanding an explanation. Instead, she presented her back to him, dismissing him with an imperious wave of her hand designed to send lackeys to their quarters.

Ty chuckled and opened the door. "I'll understand if you need more time." The door clicked shut behind him.

And Carrie issued several epithets that were most unbecoming a lady.

Carrie reached her office in twenty-nine minutes, more to prove a point than any desire to be on time. She didn't spare the tall, dark man at her side a glance as she stuck the key in the lock and opened her offices. She moved through the dim hallways, switching on lights. She could feel his eyes on her, watching her every move, like a trained spy. It unnerved her. "My office is the last door on the right. I'll be there shortly."

Ty waited in the hallway until she reappeared. "I'd rather you lead the way."

"Scared of getting lost?" She queried sweetly.

"I don't make first entrances, hazards of the job."

"So if there's a bomb in the room, you're not going to be the first toasted, right?"

His lips twitched. "Something like that."

He had a beautiful smile. Irritated with herself for noticing, Carrie hit the light switch on the wall in her office with more force than necessary. "Have a seat, Mr. Hamilton and I hope that we can make this meeting as quick as possible. I was being truthful when I said I had other plans."

"I never doubted your sincerity, Ms. Winslow." Ty waited until she was seated before he sat down opposite her. His large figure made her office shrink. Even the large, teakwood desk separating them seemed to fade in the face of his imposing figure.

Clearing her throat slightly, Carrie folded her hands atop the desktop and met his gaze directly. "Well?"

Facing her in the light provided by the twin lamps on either side of her desk, Ty's attention was riveted by the shape and beauty of her face. Perfectly symmetrical, her features were perfect. Soft brown eyes were set in a flawless face that was offset by perfectly arched eyebrows and full, sexy lips. Her dark hair was highlighted with auburn accents that seemed to catch the light as she moved. Long and silky, it fell to just below her shoulders. She wore it tucked behind her ears; the cut was perfect for her face. Ty allowed himself the luxury of admiring her beauty for a minute longer, pleased that the curvaceous body he caught a glimpse of inside the spa didn't overshadow the face. They were a perfect match. Caroline Winslow was a beautiful woman and Ty didn't give compliments very easily...even to himself.

"Mr. Hamilton, are you going to tell me what you wanted to talk about or are you going to continue to stare at me?"

Ty smiled. "It's possible to do both. You're a very attractive woman."

Carrie's breath caught in her throat. She wasn't easily caught off guard. Her tongue darted out to lick her lips, helping her to stall for time before she could formulate a proper response. Her mother's indignation would demand an apology for daring to voice such an incredibly sexist opinion. But being the daughter that she was, Carrie didn't usually follow her mother's dictates, even the lessons she'd been taught through the years. She found herself dipping her head and responding with a soft, "thank you."

Ty leaned back in the chair, folding one ankle over his knee. "I've embarrassed you. I'm sorry. I just imagined that you were used to hearing such compliments...unless there's a lot of blind men in Peking."

Carrie laughed slightly. "We don't have any blind men in Peking."

He liked her smile, her soft laughter and his body responded with a powerful kick that had him shifting positions. "Surely, they can't be immune to your beauty."

Carrie picked up a pen and threaded it through her fingers. "I'm sure you didn't want to continue this conversation in private to discuss my looks."

Full lips parted to reveal even, white teeth. "You're right." His smile faded into seriousness that got Carrie's full attention. "I'm afraid you have a criminal living among you...a very dangerous criminal. He's wanted by the federal government for conspiracy to commit murder, money laundering, assault with a deadly weapon and many other charges that I won't go into, many which involve federal agents. His name is Jake Spencer. Do you know him?"

Carrie breathed a sigh of relief. "No. I'm happy to say I think you have the wrong town."

"I don't think so. He's obviously using an alias. We expected as much." He opened the manila folder he'd brought with him and removed the full-size photograph. "This is the Jake Spencer we know and we have every reason to believe that he is here in your town."

Carrie felt the blood drain from her face as she stared at the well-known visage. "This can't be possible. The man in this photograph is no criminal. Believe me, Mr. Hamilton," she handed the glossy picture back to him, "I make my living dealing with criminals and crooks. I know one when I see one. That man is no criminal."

"What's his name here?"

Carrie shook her head. "I'm not about to disrupt a man's life simply because you believe he's Jake Spencer. If you want me to believe you, then you're going to have to provide me with a hell of a lot more evidence than just a photograph and a..." The manila folder hit the top of her desk, interrupting Carrie's stream of heated words. Her gaze fell to the papers lying face up for her inspection. Long, slender fingers curved around the edge of the first sheet, her eyes widening as she scanned the condemning words. "This can't be true." She dropped the paper and covered her face with her hands. "How could he...how is this possible?"

"Ms. Winslow, I know this can't be easy for you. You've had six months to get to know a man that you like, respect even, and now to discover that he's wanted by the federal government, well, it can be devastating." His voice was soothing, calming, but Carrie was in no mood to be soothed.

She pushed herself away from her desk and climbed to her feet. "No. Stop." She lifted one hand and backed toward the door. "I know that man in that picture and no matter what he may have done in his past, he isn't a criminal any longer."

"Are you willing to stake your life on that and possibly the lives of your friends? He's hired men to kill his enemies. What happens if one of your family members piss him off? Are you going to take the chance that he really is a changed man?" Ty got to his feet as well, approaching her, trapping her against the far wall beside the door. "Maybe you haven't thought about the consequences of your actions, but I have and unfortunately, this isn't your decision to make. I came here to find Jake Spencer, or whatever his name is here. And I'll find him with or without your help." He spun away from her and reached for the doorknob.

"Wait." Unwittingly, she caught hold of his forearm, capturing his attention. "I do know him. His name is Jarod Deming and he's...dating my best friend." She lowered her gaze to her wine-colored fingernails resting against his dark skin. "I still don't want to believe what you're telling me."

He covered her hand with his. "I know, but it's true. I didn't come here to cause trouble; I came to end it before it can begin. It's very important that you not saying anything to Jarod. You can't let on like you know the truth." When she didn't look back up at him, he bent his knees to see her face. "Caroline, listen to me. It's beyond important; it's imperative. Promise me that you aren't going to say anything to him."

Carrie met his hazel-eyed gaze, catching her breath at the intensity of his gaze. For a brief second, a quick flash of time, she wondered if the man was as intense in everything he did. She realized his hand was still covering hers and she quickly yanked it away, tucking her hands behind her back. "Of course I won't say anything. You're going to arrest him today anyway, right? I mean, it will be over in a matter of a few hours and then I won't have to worry about keeping quiet, right?" With his silence, she prompted him. "Right?"

"Not exactly." Ty dropped his gaze and Carrie's internal alarm went off. She'd defended too many guilty men to know when one was tiptoeing around the truth.

"What does that mean? You know who he is. You should just arrest him and get it over with, let this town heal. A lot of people here care for Jarod and he's become an integral part of our society. My best friend is in love with him and I think he's in love with her. And you're telling me that you're not going to arrest him now that you know where he is? Isn't that what you wanted from me, to know his alias, where he was? Well, I've given you his name and as far as where he is, I can only assume he's at work on Mrs. Grady's house as he's the town's only handyman. I can get you her address if you'd like to wait." She tried to side-step around him but his hand shot out, closed around her wrist.

"Wait."

Her eyes narrowed. "And exactly what am I waiting for, Mr. Hamilton?"

"It's a complicated situation." He hedged.

"That's it? That's all you're going to tell me? Maybe you don't understand what I'm telling you, Mr. Hamilton, so let me make it clearer. This is going to devastate a lot of people." She peeled his fingers away from her skin and whirled away from him, putting the desk back between them. "You can't begin to imagine how close many people have gotten to this man. We've had him in our homes. We've enjoyed dinners with him, made friends with him and now, suddenly, you're standing here telling me that he's a criminal, but that you're not going to arrest him immediately. The least you can do is tell me why."

Ty walked toward her, rounded the desk and much to her surprise, settled his large hands on her shoulders. "I wish I could tell you more, but I can't. Much of the information that I have is classified and you don't have the clearance."

"Oh, let me guess, you could lose your job."

"Yes."

"I don't even know you and I'm supposed to believe you?"

"You don't have to believe me. Call the agency. They will tell you who I am and why I'm here. I have nothing to hide."

"Except the reason why you won't arrest Jarod."

"Jake Spencer. His name is Jake Spencer."

Carrie lowered her eyes to the strong column of his throat, realizing just how close he was standing to her a split second before her telephone jangled. She jumped, caught her breath and stumbled back against her desk. His hands reached out to save her from crashing to the floor. It was the second time that day he'd kept her upright, saved her dignity. For some reason, the thought irritated her. She took it out on her caller.

"Yes?"

"I thought you were going to take the day off," Jennifer's voice was slightly accusing.

Carrie felt the blood drain from her face. Jennifer. What was she supposed to say to her? "I-I had something to take care of."

"It didn't have anything to do with that gorgeous man who rolled into town late last night, does it? Folks at the diner said he was asking about you. Do you know him?"

"Hmm?" Carrie tried to think of an appropriate response. She could feel Ty's eyes boring into the side of her face, making her uncomfortable. "Oh, damn, Jen, there goes the other line. Let me call you back in a few minutes, okay?" She disconnected the line before her friend could object. Then, slamming the receiver back into the cradle, she rounded on her visitor. "That was my best friend, Jennifer, the one that happens to be dating your criminal. I didn't know what to say to her. I've never had that problem before. Do you want to tell me how I'm supposed to tell her that the man she's currently dating is not the type of man she wants to piss off?" Her brown eyes were blazing, her shoulders shaking with the force of her emotions. Trembling legs carried her around the desk to put some distance between them. "Let me think. Oh, yes, I could always just say, 'by the way, Jen, if I were you, I wouldn't be making any long terms plans with Jarod. You see, he isn't Mr. Right, after all.' No? Too sappy? You're right. Maybe I should just be bold and tell her to run for her life while she still can. Or perhaps there's a reward out for his arrest. Maybe the last six months of her life won't be a total loss." She tossed her hands up in the air. "I'm open to suggestions, Mr. Hamilton."

His eyes performed a slow study of her face with characteristic thoroughness before he responded to her hysterical tirade. "I would suggest you introduce me to your friend and Mr. Spencer. To them, I am your friend, someone you met in law school. For now, you tell Jennifer nothing. A woman would find it very difficult to hide anything from the man that she loves. You could be putting your friend's life in danger if you tell her the truth."

Carrie walked away from him, eager to put as much distance between them as possible. She reached the door and flung it open, keeping her back to him. "This is great. Perfect. I'm supposed to lie to the woman who's known me since the third grade. Do you know that she reads me like the morning newspaper? She knows when I'm keeping something from her. The mailman knows when I'm lying. I've never been very good at it."

Ty's long legs ate up the distance between them until he was standing inches away from her spine. "Caroline, this is probably going to be the hardest thing you've ever done, but you have to do it."

"Why? Why can't I just tell you to go to hell and pretend this conversation never even took place?"

He turned her around to face him. "Because you're too ethical. You know that you have to do the right thing here. I'm here to help make sure that you do it."

"I can't begin to tell you how much your presence alone is going to make things easier," Carrie's defense mechanism kicked in, dripping sarcasm from her tongue.

Ty smiled. "You can't go through life looking for the easy way out."

"If I wanted a philosophy lesson, I would read one of Socrates' plays." Her eyes dropped to her watch. "I need to run."

"Keep your evening free. I'll need to see you again." It was a blatant lie. In fact, his job might be simpler if he avoided Carrie Winslow altogether. He didn't need or want entanglements and the only thing his mind pictured when he saw Carrie was an entanglement...of arms, legs and sheets.

Carrie lifted her face, meeting his eyes. "I already have one father, Mr. Hamilton; I don't need another."

A father? He resisted the urge to laugh. He definitely wasn't feeling paternal. "Where do you live? I'll come by about seven." At her raised eyebrows, he continued, "We're supposed to know one another, remember? I think we need a quick cramming session of facts and personal information."

If that was a pick-up lines, it was one of the best she'd heard in a long time. She walked back to her desk and jotted her address down on a yellow post-it note. "Here. Please don't take this the wrong way, but I hope you don't stay in town very long. I want this over with as quickly as possible, for my friend's sake, for this town's sake."

Ty inclined his head slightly. "I'll do my best."

* * *

Carrie tugged her office door shut and headed down the hallway to the front foyer, hoping she could go home, sink into a tub and pretend this day never happened. "Caroline," her mother's imperious tones stopped her.

"Great. Just damned fantastic." Carrie rested her forehead against the smooth paneled wall before straightening her shoulders and responded to her mother's call. "I'm here, Mother."

"Who in the world was that man that just left here?" Carrie knew that Candace didn't believe in wasting time with preambles. Greetings and the like were reserved for people with little or nothing to say. Candace always had something to say.

Carrie pinched the bridge of her nose between her thumb and forefinger. Here would be the ultimate test of Ty Hamilton's idea. If she could fool her mother, it was possible that she could fool her best friend. The idea made her nauseous. "He's a friend...someone I met in law school."

Candace wrinkled her nose in obvious distaste. "He is a lawyer? He looked like a hoodlum."

Carrie wasn't surprised that her mother would think that. Candace was big on appearances and in his jeans and t-shirt, Ty hadn't looked like a typical lawyer. She had to think fast as she walked past her mother, switching off lights. "Well, he's neither, actually. Ty dropped out of law school in his second year."

Candace nodded her head understandingly. "Of course. That makes sense. He looked, well, a bit rough if you ask me. So why was he here? Please tell me he was not asking you for money."

Carrie smothered a laugh. The idea that a man like Ty Hamilton would ask her for money was ludicrous. The man oozed pride and self-respect. He was strong, capable and would never need to depend on someone else to pay his way in life. She frowned at her mental defense of a man she barely knew. "No, Mother, he wasn't here to ask for money. He's just passing through and thought we could catch up." And rough wasn't such a bad term to describe him, either. She would imagine that he wasn't one to follow rules. He did things his way, without taking the time to consider the consequences or the fallout to the people around him.

Candace patted her smooth bob, tucked an imaginary stray hair back into place. "What is there to catch up on? You graduated from Harvard; he did not. You became a successful lawyer; he did not. There. All caught up. Did you send him on his way?"

Carrie was beginning to feel ill and wondered how she could make a dignified exit without incurring her mother's wrath. That's what it was all about, of course...going through life ensuring that Candace Winslow was happy. Stifling an hysterical giggle, she pressed her palm against her forehead and sidled toward the exit. "Mother, I'd really love to stay and continue this conversation, but I need to go home and take some aspirin."

Candace's unlined hand dipped into her handbag and she produced a bottle of pain reliever. "Now, did you send that man on his way?" Her smooth, cultured voice sharpened.

Feeling snide, Carrie tilted her face upwards and fixed her mother with a sharp stair. "Actually, we're having dinner tonight to catch up. He had another appointment, something to do with some real estate purchase. I think he's buying a piece of property here in town. Wouldn't that be wonderful? He could end up living right next to you and Dad. That property is for sale, isn't it, Mother? Oh, and I think he owns a Harley." Carrie managed to make it all the way to the glass door this time while her mother was busy picking her chin up off the floor. "Now, I really need to lock up."

Candace traveled toward her daughter on high heels that would have been more at home at a gala function than Carrie's simple office. "You are having dinner with that...that...man? He was wearing torn jeans and...sneakers...in the middle of the day. He looked destitute. And very much out of place. Your father would never approve of him, Caroline."

Carrie sighed heavily. "Mother, I'm having dinner with him; I'm not having his child."

Candace gasped aloud and then clapped a hand over Carrie's mouth while sliding a covert glance around to see if she'd been overheard. "That simply is not funny! Having his child, indeed! You do not even know the man all that well."

"And we both know that's not really what's bothering you." Carrie smiled sweetly. "It's not the fact that he may be common or the fact that he's not a lawyer or that I might not know him well enough. What you're really thinking, Mother, is that he's not my kind, right?"

Candace continued to sneak looks around. "I simply do not know what you are talking about. You know your father would disapprove of your dating a man that was not in your league."

"Well, let's see, he drives a Porsche, makes probably ten times more a year than I do; he's single, good-looking, well-mannered and oh, yes, he's a man." Carrie's hands smacked the sides of her legs. "From where I'm standing, those qualities put him in my league. I'm searching for the problem that you have with him because I'm sure that neither one of my parents look down their noses at anyone. That's just not good manners, Mother." With her hand at the small of her mother's back, she ushered her out into the late morning sunshine. "Now, if you will excuse me, I need to go. I'll see you and Dad later on this week." Locking the door behind her, she made good her escape, leaving Candace to consider her last paragraph.

* * *

Carrie opened her door before Ty could ring the doorbell. "You're early." She accused with an approving look at his casual attire of black jeans and white buttoned-down shirt. "Don't you own a suit?" She was still feeling the sting of her mother's condemnation.

Ty grinned, obviously unperturbed by her hostility. "Do you always greet your guests like that?"

"Only those who invite themselves over." Spinning on her heel, she walked into the living room, leaving him to follow or stand in the doorway for the rest of the evening."

"Why, thank you, Caroline, I would love to come in."

She turned, facing him. "Carrie."

"What?"

"My name is Carrie to all of my friends. Only my parents insist on calling me Caroline."

"And my friends call me Ty, but you haven't yet."

"I'm still getting used to the idea that we're supposed to be friends." She plopped down on the sofa and indicated the chair opposite her with a wave of her hand. "Have a seat."

He sat down beside her, so close the denim material of his jeans brushed against her bare leg. "I know this is going to be a challenge for you."

Carrie shifted away from the heat of his body. "A challenge is when I walk into the courtroom. This is more of a nightmare."

"I can make it easier for you if you'll let me."

She almost shivered at the intensity in his voice. "You're the one that brought this into my life. The only way you could make it easier is to arrest Jarod...Jake now."

"I can't do that."

"Why am I not surprised?" She got to her feet, running nervous hands down the front of her simple, black miniskirt, wishing she'd worn something that offered more coverage. When she'd chosen the skirt and cropped, white t-shirt, she'd needed the boost of confidence the outfit gave her, but now, standing in front of this man with the sexy hazel eyes and knowing smile, she wanted to dive for her bedroom and wrap herself in the thick quilt covering her bed. He was watching her, peeling away layers of her defenses and she was attracted to him, more than she had ever been to any man, attracted enough to want him to stay. "Would you like a drink?"

"Anything non-alcoholic."

Carrie surveyed the contents of her refrigerator. "I have Coke, orange juice, milk, tea, cranberry juice..."

"Coke is fine," Ty was standing right behind her; she could feel the heat of his body closer to hers.

Her hands fumbled with the can of soda; Ty quickly rescued it and placed it on the counter top.

"Are you frightened of me, Carrie?"

"Of course not." Her voice came out in a high-pitched squeal that gave him the correct answer. "I don't have any reason to be afraid of you, do I? I mean just because I don't know you and I've let you into my home doesn't mean I should be afraid of you, right?"

He touched her shoulder with his hand, but didn't let it linger. "You have no reason to fear me. I'm not here to hurt you. I'm only here to talk, to get to know you so that your friends think I know you."

"Right. My friends." She opened the refrigerator door once more and pulled out the carton of orange juice.

"You'd better let me do that for you. The way your hands are shaking, you'll probably miss the glass altogether."

Carrie didn't argue. In fact, she was grateful. She stuffed her shaking hands behind her back and tried to find something to do with the rest of her body so that she didn't appear blatantly nervous. "I lied." The words were out before she could catch them. She lied? Where that come from? Great. He was looking at her now, one eyebrow lifted, one hand extended holding a glass of orange juice that there was no possible way that she was going to be able to drink.

"How so?" His voice wasn't condemning, just curious.

It gave Carrie courage to continue. "I am a little scared of you, but not because I think you're going to hurt me."

His laugh poured over her like warm whiskey. He took hold of her arm and guided her back toward the living room as if she needed assistance to make it through the rooms of her own house. "That was information I already had, Carrie." She liked the way he said he name, with just the right amount of inflection, enough to make it sound sensual.

She sank down onto the sofa and drew the green and white checked afghan over her knees. "It's just been a while since I had a man call me beautiful and you did today and then you looked at me like you wanted to…" she broke off, horrified at the path her mind had taken.

His lips twitched. "How long has it been since you've had sex, Carrie?"

She should be offended at the question, but her heart was racing too fast. She tucked a strand of hair behind her ear and looked away. "Do you think we could change the subject?"

"You find me attractive and knowing that I think you're beautiful is unnerving to you." His hand reached out, captured the glass of orange juice and set it down on the table in front of them.

"I-I didn't say that. I was generalizing," Carrie held her hands up to ward off his intentions, although she wasn't really sure of what they were.

He placed his Coke beside her juice and scooted closer on the sofa. "So you don't find me attractive then?"

"I thought you were here to learn about my friends, about me."

"I am and what better way to learn about someone than to discover the way they kiss? You can tell a lot about a person from the way they respond to you. If they melt," he lifted a hand and brushed his knuckles down her cheek, softly, a lover's caress, "if they sigh against your lips," his hand moved to the long, smooth line of her neck, "or if they whisper your name. Would you whisper my name, Carrie?"

Carrie's lids slid to half-mast and she heard herself catch her breath as he moved even closer to her. She couldn't whisper his name because her throat had closed, making speech impossible. His jeans burned against her leg; his hands resting on either side of her hips. She opened her eyes wider and discovered he was lowering his head, his lips seconds away from touching hers. She should stop him, back away, but she was frozen and she couldn't think of one reason why she should stop him.

His lips brushed hers once, twice and then he backed off, his eyes meeting hers. The silence in the room was almost deafening as their gazes locked. Tension clawed its way up Carrie's spine and she held her breath, waiting for him to make the next move. She didn't have long to wait.

Hooking his hand behind her head, Ty pulled her closer, fusing his lips to hers in a kiss that was anything but hesitant. Powerful emotions churned inside of him, emotions like desire, passion, and a longing so intense his knees went weak. He could taste the orange juice, her fear, and her surrender. And deep inside, close to his heart, he wanted her. That's what made him pull away, stand up, put some distance between them. His breath came in rapid succession and he walked away, presenting his back to her line of vision.

"I'm sorry. I shouldn't have done that." His voice was hoarse.

Carrie fell back against the cushion, closing her eyes. "Probably not." Her own breath came just as labored.

He turned, fixed her with another surveying look. "We're supposed to be just friends."

With her eyes still closed, Carrie's fingers touched her tingling lips. "I don't think I've ever kissed my friends like that."

He massaged the back of his neck and focused his attention on his shoe tops. "Should I leave?"

Carrie's eyes popped open. "I thought we were supposed to get to know one another."

"I think we both learned something about ourselves that we weren't ready for."

Carrie nodded slowly. "I'm attracted to you."

A punch in the stomach would have been easier to take. He rocked back on his heels and met her gaze once more. "And I'm attracted to you, but I'm here to do a job. Nothing can interfere with that job."

"And nothing will. Just because we're attracted to each other, Ty, doesn't mean that we have to act on that attraction."

He gave her an almost pitying glance. "We were alone five minutes just now. That was all it took. We're going to be spending a lot of time together."

Carrie held up one hand. "Please. I think I can control myself."

Could he? He wondered. "Okay. We'll play it your way." He walked back toward her.

She sat up straighter and scooted toward the far end of the sofa. "Wh-what are you doing?"

He stopped. "Well, I was going to sit down, if that's okay."

She gave a nervous giggle. "Oh. Of course. I mean, that's fine." She drew the afghan tighter around her legs and folded her hands primly in her lap. The miniature grandfather clock over the mantel chimed seven o'clock and Carrie wondered how long she could maintain her dignity before she leaped across the cushions and flung herself into Ty's muscled arms. She tamped down another giggle and plastered a smile on her face. "Okay, so what do you want to know first?"

Everything. Anything. He wanted to know what made her laugh, what made her cry and what she wanted most in the world. But most of all, he wanted to know what sounds she would make when he made love to her. Would she whisper his name in a hesitant plea or would she cry it aloud as her climax wrapped around her. He swallowed hard, trying to focus on her question. Without any idea how, he replied with a calm, "why don't you tell me about college?"

"My mother thinks you dropped out of law school."

Ty leaned forward, dropping his hands down between his knees. "Why does your mother know anything about me?"

"She came to visit me after you left. She wanted to know who you were."

"And you told her that we met in college and that I dropped out? Thanks." He gave her a crooked smile. "I don't know whether to be grateful that you think quickly on your feet or offended that you turned me into a hoodlum in your mother's eyes."

Carrie waved a hand in dismissal. "Oh, that. You were a hoodlum long before I ever said anything. Mother has a problem with any man dressed in scruffy jeans and a t-shirt in the middle of the day. If you're not wearing a suit and tie, you're either a construction worker or a hoodlum."

Ty laughed, a deep, throaty laugh that started a low burn in Carrie's stomach. "Nice. I think I'm looking forward to meeting your parents."

Carrie shot him a horrified glance. "You're not going to meet my parents! That's out of the question. My father would see through this charade! He reads people too well."

"Did I mention that I'm an undercover operative, Carrie? I make my living convincing people that I'm who and what I say I am. I think I can handle your parents."

Famous last words, she thought glumly. "Just remember that I warned you."

Chapter Three

"Hey, you! Where have you been keeping yourself these last two days? I've been trying to call you, but there's been no answer." Jennifer plunked herself down into the leather chair opposite her best friend's desk. "So what's going on?"

Carrie blew a thick lock of sable hair out of her eyes and propped her elbows on top of a thick manila file folder. "I've just been busy. Trying to catch up after my two days' vacation which I never should have taken."

Jennifer crossed slim legs and narrowed her eyes. "And your 'busyness' wouldn't have anything to do with a certain, tall, handsome stranger that blew into town a few days ago, would it? I believe I asked you about him at your office a couple of days ago and you blew me off. Have you been seeing him? Your parents will flip. I heard that he's not the white-collar type."

Carrie's brows knitted in a frown. "What does that mean?"

"Hmm? Well, it means that he's not the suit and tie type of guy."

"So what's wrong with that?"

"I didn't say there was anything wrong with it. Why are you getting so defensive? Is there something you aren't telling me?" Jennifer leaned forward, an avaricious gleam in her eyes. "Oh my God, you've been seeing him, haven't you? Why didn't I suspect? I should have realized that's the reason why you've been avoiding me! This is great! I want to meet him. How do you know him? Or did you just meet him, too? Is he really as gorgeous as people in town have been saying?"

Carrie's eyes strayed to the open door of her office and she sighed heavily. "Why don't you turn around and look for yourself?" She dropped her head into her hands and groaned.

Jennifer whipped around so quickly she almost fell out of the chair. Recovering quickly, she bounced to her feet, hand extended. "Hi. I'm Jennifer Braddock, Carrie's best friend. I was hoping to get the opportunity to meet you."

Ty captured her hand in his and returned her smile. "It's a pleasure to meet you as well. I'm Ty Hamilton."

"At least now I can see why Carrie's been keeping you all to herself. You're absolutely gorgeous."

"Thank you." He slid a smile toward Carrie. "Actually, Carrie and I were making plans to introduce me to her friends this weekend."

"So she has been keeping you under wraps, enjoying the fruits of her secrecy while the rest of us are in the dark. How long have the two of you been seeing one another?" Jennifer was almost drooling.

Ty cupped his chin in his hand and appeared deep in thought. "I think it's been about three months now but this is the first chance I've had to visit her here. Usually, she comes to Atlanta to see me." The lies flowed smoothly from his forked tongue while Carrie sat behind her desk, her mouth open and a stunned expression on her face.

Jennifer clapped her hands delightedly. "I knew there was a reason why she was so fascinated with Atlanta. Do you know how many continuing legal education classes she's taken in that city since the beginning of the year? Oh, what am I saying? Of course you do. Only, she was furthering her education in a different way, wasn't she?" Turning, she planted her hands on her hips and gave her best friend a mock scowl. "I can't believe you kept this a secret from me."

"Maybe because it wasn't a secret." Carrie muttered through gritted teeth. "Ty and I are friends."

"We were friends first," he corrected neatly.

Jennifer's eyes were glazing with excitement. "This is wonderful! All this time I've felt guilty at finding happiness with Jarod and here you've found a little something all for yourself. Only," she threw a wicked glance over her shoulder, "it's not exactly little."

Ty shifted beneath the woman's bold scrutiny. "Let's hope not."

"Why don't we just ask Carrie?" Jennifer chuckled.

Carrie's hands smacked the top of her desk as she got to her feet. "Why don't we not? You," she pointed a finger toward her best friend, "out! I've got work to do and you," her finger swept toward Ty, "I have a bone to pick with you."

His eyebrows arched. "Interesting turn of phrase."

Carrie could feel the color rushing to her face and she whipped around to regain control before she began screeching like a trapped hyena. Taking deep, calming breaths she'd learned in her Yoga class, she finally managed to focus her attention on the couple still standing inches away. "Jen, I'd like to be alone with Ty, if you don't mind."

"I'll bet you would." Jennifer crab-walked toward the door. "I'll tell your secretary that you need a little alone time." She winked broadly. The door slammed shut behind her.

Carrie rounded on the incredibly handsome, impossibly smug man facing her. "How dare you! That wasn't part of our agreement! We were supposed to be friends not...not..."

"Lovers?" He supplied helpfully.

"Exactly! How could you...what were you thinking?"

"That it would explain the sexual tension between us."

Her anger deflated like a ten-day old balloon. He had a point...a big point. The past two days had been difficult to say the least. Now, at least, if she touched him, accidentally, of course, she wouldn't have to worry about what people were thinking. They would assume that she was, that they were... she slid him a glance from beneath lowered lids. And would they? She shivered in spite of the heat in the room. "I just don't think it was the best course of action. Jennifer can't keep a secret."

"Then," he wrapped one arm around her waist and tugged her close to his muscled frame, "it's about time we came out of the dark." Dipping his head, he caressed her lips with his.

Carrie jerked and pressed her palms against the solid wall of his chest. "We can't do this. What about your job? Your reason for being here? You have to remain centered, remember?"

He cupped her face with his large hands. "The man I've come to arrest isn't here right now. At this moment, it's just you and me. And I want to kiss you."

Carrie's hands curled around his wrists. "Okay."

Carrie could feel the eyes on her when she walked into the diner. Somehow, she managed to make it to the back of the room with her dignity still intact. Sitting down opposite her best friend, she narrowed her eyes into a threatening glare. "You've been talking."

Jennifer lifted her shoulders in a sheepish shrug. "What was I supposed to say when people asked me about the two of you? You know I've never been very good at lying."

"Except when it was to save your sorry hide." She slumped down lower in the chair until her knees rested against the edge of the table. "I'm not sure I can handle this."

Jennifer beamed. "Of course you can. Besides, what's to handle? You're dating a handsome, eligible man who..."

"Just happens to come up lacking on my parents' social register. Mother doesn't like it that Ty dropped out of law school."

"So what does he do now?"

Carrie was stymied. They hadn't discussed what Ty's current occupation was supposed to be. "Do?"

"Yes, as in work, how does he make ends meet?"

Carrie said the first thing that came to mind. "He doesn't really."

"You mean he's unemployed?" Jennifer clapped her hands together and squealed her delight. "Oh, this is priceless! I'd love to be a fly on the wall to see your mother's face when you tell her that he doesn't have a job."

"Well, I didn't really have any intentions of..."

"You have to tell them! It'll be fantastic!" Jennifer's eyes were alit with excitement. "Could you try to do it when Jarod and I are there?"

"Well, I didn't really mean that he was..."

Jennifer held up a hand to cut her off. "You don't have to explain anything to me, Carrie. I'm on your side, remember? And since when did what your parents think bother you? If I remember correctly, you dated Mike Hammond when you were in college and he was the waiter at one of the restaurants. Your parents found out; they hit the roof and yet, you continued to date him." Jennifer continued to smile. "He must have been some guy."

"No," Carrie corrected glumly, "it was out of spite. I knew my parents would disapprove. I dated Mike because I wanted to prove to them that I was no longer under their thumb. I think I hurt him."

"Oh, he's probably not even thinking about it now." Jennifer folded her hands atop the table, a considering look on her face. "Either that or he's spent the last four or five years plotting your demise and he'll be here any day to make good on his plan."

Carrie rolled her eyes. "Ty is different from any guy I've ever dated."

"You mean because he's intelligent, strong and doesn't let you run over him."

"Oh, the last part he wouldn't mind...if we were horizontal." Carrie responded with a twitch to her lips. "And just so you know, we haven't slept together."

"I heard that unspoken yet."

Carrie didn't bother to deny it. "Oh, he would tonight if I said yes."

"So what's keeping you from saying yes?"

How about the fact that she'd only known him for two days? "Caution, I guess. I've had too many disastrous relationships to even consider the fact that this one could make it."

"You're attracted to him; he's obviously attracted to you. I say quit beating around the bushes and hit the rose bed, so to speak." She flashed an engaging grin.

Carrie chuckled. "It's been tough."

"Dating him?"

"No, keeping myself from dragging him down the hall and into my bedroom. Every night, when he's preparing to leave, I want to just throw myself into his arms and beg him not to go."

"I doubt that you would have to beg."

Carrie inclined her head and smiled at her hands, knowing the truth behind her friend's words. In the past two days, the tension had escalated to a palatable level and she was sure an implosion was imminent.

Jennifer squealed with laughter, then with a quick glance around, lowered her voice. "Well, I want to know everything when you finally do hit the sack with this guy. I mean, I want all of the gory, intimate details. The guy is," her face took on a dreamy quality, "well, I don't need to tell you. How does he kiss?"

Carrie's fingers automatically touched her lips, still slightly swollen from Ty's last kiss less than an hour before. How did he kiss? How could she describe it? She didn't think the usual adjectives would do it justice. With just the touch of his lips, the man leveled her consciousness, pushed away all descending thoughts and replaced them with a powerful explosion of emotions, colors, and contexts that made her want to cling to him, hold him, and beg him to stay. She'd been right; there were no adjectives that could do the job properly. She settled for a serene smile coupled with a "fine."

Jennifer propped her elbows on the table and dropped her head into her cupped hands. "Please don't disappoint me by telling me that Ty Hamilton, looking like he does, only kisses fine. You can do better than that. I've been to court. I've heard you wax eloquent about a farmer's crop. I know that you can call upon your repertoire of glowing words and come up with something more befitting a man with Ty's abilities. So come on, I'm waiting." She waggled her fingers in anticipation.

In spite of the red creeping up her neck, Carrie opted for honesty. "I can't even begin to describe it, Jen. All I can say is that I've never been kissed like that before. He touches me."

Jennifer's jaw hung slack; her eyes glazed and she responded with a marveled, "wow."

The bell jangled over the door, drawing attention to the entering customer. Sharon's face lit up and she practically vaulted over the counter top in her eagerness to reach the man. "Well, hello, Mr. Hamilton. It's so nice to see you again. Would you like a table?"

Ty's eyes scanned the room, landed on Carrie's dark head and he gave the owner a smile. "Thank you, but I'm meeting someone." He touched her shoulder briefly and walked toward the far corner of the room.

Jennifer's eyes flitted toward the center of the room and she caught her breath. "Oh, Lord, here he comes."

Carrie straightened seconds before Ty reached their table. "Hi." Her hands went to her hair and she wished she'd taken the time to run a brush through the tangled strands before she'd escaped to the diner.

Ty's eyes dropped to her lips before he replied. "Hi." He trained his gaze on Jennifer's glowing face "It's good to see you again, Jennifer."

As if poked in the rear with a sharp instrument, Jennifer leaped to her feet. "Oh, yeah, well, I've got to run. I'm supposed to meet Jarod in," she checked her watch for effect, "ten minutes. I'll call you later, Carrie. Ty, nice to see you, too." Her booted feet slapped against the tile as she made her way through the throng of customers.

Ty swiveled a gaze back toward Carrie. "Something I said?"

"No, she really did have to meet Jarod. Have a seat." Carrie wondered why he was here and what on earth she was going to tell her mother when this got back to her. And there was no doubt in her mind that it would get to her mother's ears. Candace Winslow had listening devices in every corner of Peking. She couldn't sneeze without her mother calling her to find out if she had a cold.

"You ran out of your office as if someone had just yelled fire." Ty sat down across from her, scooting the chair back to accommodate his greater height.

Carrie lowered her eyes to her hands, decided that she needed a manicure, and slid her gaze toward the salt and pepper shakers at the far end of the table. "I-I needed some air." Her head lifted and she quickly corrected the statement, "not because of what we were doing but because of what...we...were...doing," she finished lamely. "I mean, I didn't need oxygen. I just needed a break, a chance to clear my head." Leaning forward, she lowered her voice and confronted the situation head on. "You shouldn't kiss me like that."

He folded his arms across his chest and raised one eyebrow. "Like what?"

Carrie's heart thumped against the wall of her chest. "Like you want to...to..."

"Yes?" He wasn't going to give her a break.

She took a deep breath and plunged in. "Like you want to take me to bed."

His arms dropped, one hand reached across the table and covered one of hers. "But I do want to take you to bed."

From behind her, a coffee cup clattered against the tiled floor, shattering into a million tiny shards that would send Sharon into a fit of anger. There was a mumbled apology at the attention and Carrie closed her eyes. Forget explaining Ty's presence to her mother; explaining his last sentence was going to be even tougher.

"You're obviously not used to living in a small town, Ty. You can't just blurt out whatever is on your mind."

"You're an adult, Carrie. Why do you care what people think about you?"

"Because I have a reputation to consider."

"And you think that people will think less of you if they know that you have an active sex life?"

"They don't need to know anything about my sex life!"

"Do you have one?" He queried blatantly.

Her mouth fell open. "I'm not a virgin, if that's what you're asking."

"It wasn't, but thanks for the information. I'm asking if you're seeing anyone."

"Obviously, I'm not or I wouldn't be like this with you."

"And how are you with me?"

She fidgeted with a stack of sugar packets. "You unnerve me. You walk into the room and I can't even think." She fixed her steady gaze on his handsome face. "No man has ever taken away my ability to form a coherent sentence before."

He brought her fingers to his lips and kissed each tip. "And no woman has ever taken away my desire to leave before. So I guess we're even."

"I'm not ready to just jump into bed with you."

His eyes twinkled. "Not yet, but soon." He pressed his index finger against her full lips. "We'll both know when you're ready."

"Should I even ask about when you'll be ready?"

He grinned. "You wouldn't like my answer."

"What happened to having to keep your attention focused on your job?" Her voice was an urgent hiss.

"Right now, you are my job."

"Me?" Her eyebrows lifted. "Since when did this become about me?"

"You're in this with me."

"Not by choice."

"Do you really still want me to leave?" The taunting words were enough to propel her to her feet. He caught hold of her wrist, unmindful of the watching eyes. "You're not always going to be able to run away when you don't like a conversation, Carrie."

"I'm not running away. I'm walking and it has nothing to do with the conversation. It's more to do with the company." She shouldered her purse strap and walked toward the door, ignoring the inquiring looks and stunned faces.

"Why haven't you arrested him yet?" Dave Berringer, Agent-in-Charge and Ty's supervisor, growled into the phone.

Ty tossed his white shirt onto the foot of the bed and reached for a clean, blue t-shirt. "He hasn't given me what I need." Placing the phone atop his discarded shirt, he let the divisional director ramble on about protocol and policy before he tucked the receiver between his ear and his shoulder. "When he gives me what I'm looking for, I can arrest him and be on my way."

"You're a fool if you think he still has the money."

"Then I'm a fool, but the man hasn't gone into hiding for nothing, Berringer. He's trying to wait for the air to clear before he can take his fortune and escape the country and I think he has plans to take someone with him."

"You mean as a hostage?" Dave's voice had risen an octave.

"No, as a wife." Ty tucked the shirt into his jeans and scooped his keys off the hotel dresser. "I've got to run. I'll call you when I have more information."

"You haven't called me yet and you've been there three days!"

"Has it been that long?"

"Hell, yes, it's been that long and the brass is on my tail and they want answers. Now, what am I supposed to tell them?"

"Tell them you haven't heard from me." Ty switched the phone off and tossed it back on the bed on his way out of the room.

Seated in her office, Carrie saw her mother's approach from the corner of her eye and held up one hand to silence the tirade before it could start. It was obvious that Candace Winslow was on a mission and wasn't about to be deterred. With the phone against her ear, Carrie swiveled her chair, presenting her back to the door where Candace stood. "My assistant is finishing up the complaint now and she should be sending that out to you today. Right. I understand. Well, you have a good day, Mr. Boatwright. I'll talk to you soon." Turning back around, she returned the receiver to its cradle and waved her mother into her office. "Mother, what brings you here?" As if she really had to ask. The light of battle in Candace's eyes didn't speak well of her mother's visit. She prepared herself for the worst.

Candace walked into the office, her back ramrod straight. In the most scathing of tones, she gave the reason for her uninvited visit. "Are you dating that...that...college dropout?"

Carrie's eyebrows rose and she steepled her fingers while considering the question and her answer. "Why? What have you heard?"

Her ears practically spewing steam, Candace approached her daughter's desk. Placing her palms face down on the polished top, she leaned over until she was eye to eye. "Do not play games with me, Caroline. You know that people talk in this town. Now, I came here for answers and answers are exactly what I am going to get. Now, I will ask you once more. Are you dating that college dropout?"

Carrie sighed and rubbed the back of her neck. "I don't think it's wise to discuss my love life with you, Mother. After all, you'd only disapprove."

"Then you are dating him!"

"Carrie," Andrea Valentine, Carrie's efficient legal assistant, called to her boss through the speakerphone.

Grateful for the interruption, Carrie responded. "Yes, Andrea?"

"You have a visitor and...oh! He's on his way back!" Andrea replied on a breathless note.

There was no doubt in her mind who the 'he' was. On her feet, Carrie rounded her desk. "Well, it looks like you're about to get the opportunity to ask the college dropout himself." Walking to the door, Carrie flung it open. Without waiting for Ty to approach her, she greeted him out in the hallway, snatching a handful of his cotton shirt to tug him down to her level. With a wicked smile, she pressed her lips against his in a noisy kiss. "Hi, Baby."

Other than a slight widening of his eyes, Ty gave no indication of his surprise. Instead, he hooked an arm around her waist and drew Carrie even closer. "You call that a kiss?" Dipping his head, he slanted his lips across hers in a breath-stealing kiss. The gasps of outrage just over Carrie's shoulder didn't deter him in his quest to learn every inch of her sweet-tasting mouth. If anything, it motivated him. His hands dropping to her waist, he lifted her, holding her even with his chest.

Carrie was thankful for the support; her knees jellied, her spine wobbled and she was sure that had she been standing upright, she would have collapsed. Even as his lips plundered hers, she memorized every detail of the kiss, the firmness of his lips, the taste of coffee and mints and the scent of his skin, spice and warm male.

"You put my daughter down right this instant!" In spite of her fury, Candace somehow managed to keep her voice lower than a yell. Ladies never yelled. Ladies could speak in a forceful tone of voice, but yelling was never appropriate.

Grinning against Carrie's mouth, Ty lowered her to the floor, but continued the kiss, his hands now framing her face.

With a gurgle of dismay, Candace walked forward and lifting her purse, delivered a solid wallop against one of the man's tightly muscled arms. "I meant let her go. Get away from her."

Ty's head lifted and he fixed the woman with a slightly bored look. "I'm sorry. You are?" He felt Carrie's shoulders shake against him and he wondered if she was crying or laughing.

Candace's gaze frosted. "I am Candace Winslow, the mayor's wife and Caroline's mother. And you, young man, are in a lot of trouble."

Ty dropped his hands to Carrie's shoulders and smiled down into her upturned face. "What did I do this time, Sweetheart? I thought I'd remembered all of the appropriate anniversaries."

Carrie bit down hard on her lower lip to keep from laughing aloud. Although enjoying the scene, she knew she'd pay for her mother's outrage later. In fact, she could almost hear the phone ringing, bringing her father's point of her view. "You did." Her voice was barely above a whisper; it was all she could manage.

Hitching her purse strap over her shoulder, Candace tugged the hem of her cream, silk blouse back into place and fixed her daughter with a cold gaze. "We shall talk about this later, Caroline, when you have regained your senses....and repaired your lipstick." She favored Ty with one more disdainful glance before stalking back down the carpeted hallway.

Carrie stepped out of Ty's grasp quickly, backing into her office. "I'm sorry. I shouldn't have used you like that."

"I'm not complaining."

Suddenly very nervous, Carrie fidgeted with the paperwork on her desk. "What...um...what brings you here?"

"It's a little too late to be scared."

"It's never too late for a healthy does of fear," she corrected him.

"You're scared of me?"

"Terrified."

He folded his arms. "Why?"

She lifted her gaze. "You're kidding, right?"

The look he gave her answered her question.

"Well, just look at you," she waved a hand toward his massive chest.

His eyes dropped down the length of his body before lifting to her face once more. "My body scares you?"

His body did much more than scare her. It enticed her, intrigued her and made her mouth water, but that wasn't the answer she was going to give him. She had to put some distance between them. Of course, the action she'd just taken didn't help matters any. "Not your body exactly. You're very attractive, but I've told you that already."

"And this is a bad thing?"

Either he was being deliberately obtuse or the man was oblivious to his own sex appeal. "For the right woman, it could be a good thing."

"But you're not the right woman."

"Right."

"You are?"

"No. I'm not. I'm saying you're correct. I'm not the right woman."

"Why's that?"

"Because you're here to arrest my best friend's boyfriend."

"What has that got to do with us?"

Carrie's temples began to throb. "There is no us."

His lips twitched. "So that wasn't you with her lips fused to mine out in the hallway?"

Carrie's face flushed and she looked away from his humor-filled gaze. "You know why I kissed you."

"Because of your mother."

"Right."

He gave a light laugh. "You're lying."

She blinked at him, slightly taken aback by the blunt word. "Excuse me?"

"Your mother had nothing to do with your desire to kiss me, Carrie. In fact," Kicking the door shut, he pressed the lock before he approached her, his steps stealthy, controlled, "you still want to kiss me and you want me to kiss you. You want to feel my hands on your body, caressing your skin, sliding over your hips, your breasts." His voice dipped a notch. "You want to feel my mouth on your breasts as I taste you." He reached out one finger and slid it around the edge of her breast, watched the nipple peak in response. "And if I touched you here," his hand slid lower, cupping her through the thin material of her black slacks. He felt her body jump in response and smiled. "You would do exactly that."

Carrie's breath lodged in her throat and she closed her eyes, biting back a moan. She didn't want him. She couldn't want him. It would never work. But her body wasn't convinced.

"Why can't you just admit that you want me, Carrie? That even while denying that you're ready to 'jump into bed with me,' your body is screaming for the release that only I can give you. You want to know my body, to feel it take over yours." He was standing close to her, so close that his warm breath bathed her neck as he dipped his head. His lips slid over her throat, up near her ear, absorbing her shivers. "Tell me what you want. Say it out loud." He nibbled at her collarbone then soothed the gentle wound with a lick of his tongue.

Carrie tried to speak, to stop him, but no words would come. She tried to back away from him, but her legs wouldn't move. Her hands reached out to press against his chest, intending to push him away, but the steady thrum of his heart enticed her palms and she opened her hands to feel the wide expanse of his chest.

His fingers flexed against her sheath before sliding up to the zipper of her slacks.

Powerless to stop him, Carrie heard the rasp of the metal teeth, felt the whisper of cool air against her abdomen before the warmth of his palm sheltered her.

His fingers slid against the waistband of her bikini panties while he murmured soothing words in her ear. "Do you want me to stop, Carrie?"

Carrie's hands bunched against the fabric of his shirt and her head turned, her lips seeking his, giving him his answer more loudly than any words ever could. Without thought to their lack of privacy, she kissed him, moving her tongue against his, eager to taste him. Then his fingers found her, dipping inside the slick folds of her flesh to press against that small bud that made every nerve in her body jerk. She gasped against his lips as his fingers began a delicious assault on her senses.

Ty's lips dropped to her cheek, his tongue sliding out to caress her warm skin. "You taste like honey." His voice was thick within his throat.

She could feel the heavy weight of his cock resting against her upper thigh and her hand fell to caress him between their bodies.

He muttered a curse word and yanked her closer, his thumb pressing firmly against her clit. He could feel the muscles in her body tensing and knew she was close. He increased the tempo, drawing back to see her face, watch her eyelids close. He felt her hand cupping him and his own breathing increased.

Carrie stood on tiptoe, pulling his head back down to her face. "Take me, Ty."

His eyes widened, but he didn't ask if she was sure because she was already unzipping his jeans, freeing the heavy length of his manhood. His body surged against her palm while she stroked the dusky skin covering the tip of his shaft.

Backing with him to her desk, Carrie slid her slacks down her legs and hitched her hips onto the edge of the wood. Then her hand returned to his body, rolling over the taut skin, rubbing the dampness with her thumb. Her dark eyes glowed and she slid off the desk to drop to her knees, taking the head of his manhood into her mouth. Rolling the taste of him over her tongue, she suckled him, her hands kneading his balls gently.

Ty's hazel eyes darkened, his breath quickened and he groaned low in his throat. His hands fell to her shoulders, flexing against the soft, linen of her shirt. The muscles in his buttocks tightened and he jerked as her teeth scraped lightly over his sensitized skin.

Reaching into the back pocket of his jeans, Ty extracted a small, foil packet. Hitching his hands under Carrie's arms, he lifted her, settling her back on the edge of the desk. He unrolled the condom and slid it over the length of his penis. Then, grasping her hips, he slid her closer to him, settling himself between her splayed thighs. His eyes met hers and he thrust into her, the warmth of her body closing around him, welcoming him. With slow, steady movements, he took her, increasing the pace with each passing second, drinking in the sight of her flushed face, the way her hands curled around his wrists while her body bucked beneath his.

Carrie met his thrusts, lifting her hips off the desk to push his cock against her clit. Biting back the scream that bubbled low in her throat, she closed her eyes.

"No. Don't close your eyes," his voice was hoarse.

She obeyed his command, meeting the hazel-eyed gaze above her. "I'm close," she whispered.

"I know." His fingers tightened against her hips and leaning forward, he thrust into her once more, driving her over the edge, into a shattering climax that he silenced against his lips. His own release came within seconds and he rested his weight on his elbows, breathing hard.

Hot, damp and replete, Carrie sagged against the desktop. "Oh my God." She did close her eyes then, contentment warring with disbelief. "I've never...I don't usually..." she didn't know what to say."

He covered her mouth with his index finger. "Don't. You don't need to explain, Carrie. I know you don't make a habit of this."

Her hands cupped his face. "I've never done this before." Her face colored. "I mean, this, yes, but never in my office and certainly never with my staff just outside my door."

He chuckled lightly. "Let's just hope the intercom wasn't on."

Carrie's horrified gaze tried to see the phone just over her shoulder, but Ty pulled her up to his chest.

"Relax, it was a joke. The intercom's not on."

She relaxed against him. "It wasn't much of one."

He smiled and stroked her back before sliding his hands around to the front of her shirt.

"What are you doing?"

He unbuttoned her blouse. "Taking your shirt off."

"Why?"

"Because I want to see your breasts, but more than that, I want to taste them."

Carrie felt a languid warmth steal over her body. "I guess it's only fair considering I've already tasted you."

He slid her shirt off her shoulder. "There's more to come."

She groaned at the play on words. "Maybe I should send the girls home for the rest of the day."

"You really want them to know what we're doing in here?"

Carrie hadn't thought of that, but then, she hadn't really thought of anything since his hands began touching her, like they were doing now. She watched his dark head dip, his lips moving toward her nipple and she held her breath, waiting for that first touch of moistness against heated flesh. As his lips closed around the peak, she felt the tug in her abdomen and she barely breathed. Her hands held his head and her back arched, giving him free rein.

Ty could feel his body coming to life once more, his shaft hardening deep within the recesses of Carrie's body and he knew it was going to be a long afternoon. But he wasn't complaining.

Chapter Four

Carrie rolled over and cracked one eye open to catch a peek at the bedside clock. It was just after five in the morning and she was already alone in the bed. Stretching her aching muscles, she hummed low in her throat, her arms above her head. It had been a long afternoon, culminating into a long night that ended in her queen size bed. She'd learned every inch of Ty's marvelous body and she'd been an eager pupil, her hands never ceasing.

She lifted her palms and studied them in the dim light of the streetlight outside her window. She was sure her hands would be red, scalded from the heat of his skin. She smiled and rolled to her side, bringing her knees up close to her chest.

"Good morning," Ty murmured from the doorway.

Carrie angled a look over her shoulder and caught her breath. Leaning against the door frame, a snowy white towel curved around his neck, Ty made her mouth water. He was wearing sweat pants and nothing else, his chest glistening with either water or perspiration; Carrie wasn't sure. His long, black braids were tied back with a thick strand of leather and he was smiling at her.

She swallowed and responded on a croak. "Good morning."

"Did I wake you?" He walked into the bedroom, tossing the towel onto a nearby wicker chair.

Carrie rolled to face him fully. "No, but I knew the bed was empty."

One eyebrow rose. "After one night you're already used to me?"

"I don't think I'll ever be used to you, Mr. Hamilton. Let's just say that I wasn't ready to be without you yet. What were you doing?"

"I went for a jog and then I took a quick shower."

"How long have you been up?"

His eyes dropped to her swollen lips. "Not long enough."

Her breath caught in her throat and she saw the muscles in his abdomen tense as her eyes lowered just past his navel. "It looks like you're compensating."

He walked toward her, his breath coming slow, evenly. One knee depressed the mattress. "Has anyone ever told you that you're beautiful in the morning?"

Carrie scooted over to accommodate his body. She trailed one finger over his chest. "I believe someone may have mentioned it once or twice."

Ty couldn't begin to explain the ripples of jealously that raced down his spine. His hands cupped her face and he met her gaze.

"What's wrong?" She stared up at him.

"I'm trying not to think about those other men who've held you like this," he touched his lips to hers, "kissed you like this." He slid his body lower. "Made love to you like this."

Carrie held her breath. "No one has ever made love to me like this, Ty." She heard his low murmur of approval before his head disappeared beneath the sheet and she forgot about breathing altogether.

Whatever else Ty had mastered, he'd definitely learned the art of oral pleasure. He didn't just lick her to orgasm. He kissed, suckled, nipped and laved her, sending tiny shivers up and down her spine until she cried his name again and again. He worshipped her sheath, paid homage to her clit and when the release came, he barely gave her another moment to breathe before he claimed her again, his thick, hard shaft pushing deep into her pussy.

And Carrie couldn't think of a better way to start the day.

"So why are you so happy this early in the morning?" Yawning, Jennifer carried a fresh batch of roses to the counter and set to work arranging them into an artful display.

Carrie leaned her elbows on the counter and propped her head into her splayed hands. "My mother hates Ty."

"Your mother hates any man who isn't blue-blooded with a wallet thicker than hers. No man is ever going to be good enough to suit her...unless he bows down to her every wish. That's the way it goes, I'm afraid." Tucking a lock of soft, brown hair behind her ear, Jennifer fixed her friend with a curious look. "So how is he in bed?"

Carrie straightened. "Jennifer! I'm not about to discuss my sex life with you."

Jennifer smiled. "That's okay. You don't have to. I can see it in your eyes. You can at least tell me if he lasted for longer than the customary three minutes."

Carrie slid off the stool and walked around the flower shop, touching petals and smelling the scents. "Ummm, well, I can't imagine that I would be this sore otherwise."

"Oh, my God!" Jennifer rounded the counter and snagged her friend's arm, guiding her back. "You have to tell me everything."

"Don't you have enough to think about with Jarod?"

Jennifer's face clouded and she dropped her hand back down to her side. "I don't know what's been going on with him lately. He's distracted and," she bit her lower lip and lowered her eyes, "he hasn't lasted longer than three minutes. In fact, he acts like it's just a release to him. Then, he rolls over and wants to go to sleep. We used to talk and I..." she broke off, presenting her back to her best friend. "Maybe we shouldn't talk about this. It doesn't help matters any."

Carrie wanted to comfort her friend, but no words would come. And she knew that with the knowledge she carried, it would be dangerous to get any more involved than she already was. "I'm sorry, Jenny. Here I come with a cat-drinking-milk smile and you're miserable. I guess I should have taken a closer look at your face before I began talking about my amazing night." She settled herself back atop the cushioned stool, facing the counter.

Jennifer's face lit up. "So it was amazing."

Carrie relented. "It was incredible. The man knows almost every erogenous zone on a woman's body. Did you know that there's a spot on the back of your thighs that can make you, well, you know, when touched properly?" She grinned. "And, boy, can he touch properly."

Jennifer giggled. "Yeah, but any man can do the missionary position and come off not looking so bad. How was he in other situations, so to speak?"

Carrie squirmed beneath the scrutiny. "Well, let's just say that I lost count of the orgasms."

Jennifer sagged weakly behind the counter. "Mmm, I could live off of that for weeks. I knew when I saw those long, sexy fingers that they would drive a woman wild."

"Yeah, but did you see his tongue?" Carrie grinned impishly.

Jennifer returned the grin and forgot all about arranging the flowers. "You know tomorrow night is Jarod's birthday party. You'll still come won't you?"

A cold sliver of dread snaked its way down Carrie's spine, but she knew she couldn't let her friend down. "I guess so."

"And you'll bring Ty?"

Carrie's gaze lifted, a frown knitting her smoothly plucked eyebrows. "I'm not sure if he's going to be available."

Jennifer wouldn't take no for an answer. "Well, you just make sure that he is. I'm sure if you wiggle your hips and give him that sexy smile, he'll be more than willing to come to the party."

"For your information, I don't wiggle my hips. I..." She broke off when the cell phone in her pocket trilled. Lifting the slim black phone from the pocket of her designer purse, she clicked it open and answered the summons. "Hello."

"I've been looking for you," Ty's deep voice sent the blood singing through her veins.

Carrie's hand tightened on the phone and she answered Jennifer's questioning look with a slow nod. "I'm at Jen's flower shop. She was just reminding me about Jarod's birthday party tomorrow night. She wanted me to find out if you're available."

"I want to make love to you again," his voice lowered to a husky whisper.

Carrie almost swallowed her tongue. "I...um...well, I suppose you could let me know. She really wants you to come."

"I want you to come...like you did last night. I like to hear you scream my name."

She checked her watch, sliding off the stool. "Well, I suppose I could meet you in a few minutes. No, I don't think I have anything on my calendar today. Why don't I just meet you at my house in, say, ten minutes?"

"I'll be waiting." He replaced the receiver, leaving Carrie to deal with the aftermath of his words.

She favored her best friend with a wide smile and shouldered her purse strap. "I've got to run. Ty has something he needs to talk to me about."

"What did he say about the party?"

The party? What did he say about the party? Carrie was drawing a blank. She didn't think he'd responded to her invitation...well, at least not in the way he should have. "Oh, I think he's going to be able to make it." She shifted from foot to foot. "Now, I really have to run. It sounded kind of important."

Jennifer didn't look convinced. "There's no need to blow smoke, Carrie. I know what the 'talk' is all about, but there's probably not going to be a lot of talking involved."

Carrie hesitated at the door. "Look, if you need me to stay with you, if you need to talk some more, I can call Ty back."

Jennifer waved a hand in dismissal. "No. I'm not about to staunch your sex life just because mine's hit a snag. Just go and enjoy yourself. I'll be waiting to hear all the sordid details."

Carrie waggled her fingers in a good-bye wave, settled her sunglasses atop the bridge of her nose and headed out into the sunlight.

Her house was quiet, almost unearthly still as Carrie pushed open the front door. Tossing her purse onto the small table in the foyer, she kicked the door shut with the heel of her high-heel shoe. "Ty?" She crossed the tiled floor before she sensed his presence behind her. Whirling around, she saw him, standing beside the door, his arms folded across his naked chest. With the exception of the welcoming smile on his face, he wore nothing else.

Carrie's breath hitched in her throat. "You really were waiting for me." Releasing the top button of her silk blouse, she walked toward him.

He let her come to him, his arms remaining at his sides. "Did you doubt me?"

Her eyes scanned his muscular body, sliding down the rich, mocha skin, drinking in the sinew and strength of his taut abdomen before settling on the thick erection between his thighs. "Has any woman ever told you that you're a very beautiful man, Mr. Hamilton?"

His lips twitched as he recalled her words from that same morning. "I believe someone may have mentioned it once or twice."

She continued unbuttoning her blouse, feeling his eyes caress her skin as she bared it to his line of vision. "Yes, but have they made love to you the way I'm going to make love to you?"

He growled low in his throat. "I don't think any woman has ever made love to me the way that you do, Caroline. You love with much more than just your body. You love with your heart and soul and I can feel it all the way down to my toes."

Carrie smiled at him, that secret womanly smile that told him he hadn't seen anything yet. Her blouse slipped off her shoulders and slid to the carpeted floor in a silky heap. It was quickly followed by the creamy, lace bra that had barely shielded her full breasts from his view. She stepped out of her skirt next, rolled her panty hose down her legs and kicked off her shoes. She watched his eyes smolder with passion as she finished undressing by shimmying the ivory panties over her toned thighs.

She still stood at least a foot away from him. "So what did you have in mind for this morning?" She let one hand slide over her breasts, across her flat stomach until her fingertips reached the narrow patch of hair that covered her womanhood. She closed her eyes and tipped her head back, dipping one finger into the moistness. "Because if you don't have any ideas, I think I can come up with a few."

The hard flesh between his thighs pounded with aching intensity, but Ty didn't move. His feet were rooted to the floor as he watched her finger slide in and out of the dampness between her legs. "Lie down," he instructed hoarsely.

Carrie didn't think twice about obeying the command. She dropped to her knees before leaning her back against the plush, ivory carpet. She opened her thighs and moved her hand across the coarse hair at the apex. With her left hand, she parted the slick lips of her vagina and slid the fingers of her free hand deep inside the opening of her body. She moaned low in her throat and arched off the floor.

Ty walked toward her, his steps slow, his legs shaking. His breaths came low and deep as he watched her fingers, now wet with the fluid of her own body, sliding back and forth across the tiny bud that made her twitch with pleasure. He fell to his knees in front of her, his gaze mesmerized by the continuous movement of her fingertips. He heard her breath hitch in her throat and he swallowed hard.

Carrie stilled the movement of her fingers, her eyes still closed. "Touch me, Ty. I want to feel your fingers against me."

He didn't need a second invitation. His long fingers took over the pace, moving across the moist skin of her woman's flesh, finding her clit. He felt her body spasm beneath the rotation of his fingers; her hips lifted off the carpet and she cried out his name as she climaxed.

Before she could move, Ty's fingers moved to grasp her hips and he lowered his head, tasting of her heat and passion. His tongue moved around her clit, his teeth nibbling her flesh.

Carrie tensed and threaded her fingers through his braids, holding his head in place as his tongue darted in and out of the gate to her womanhood. She moaned his name, her muscles quivered beneath his ministrations.

Ty's hands held her thighs open while his tongue worked up and down the slick valley, drinking her juice and lavishing her with hot, wet strokes. His teeth caught the edge of her clit and he heard the quick, sharp intake of her breath and her pleas for release. Her body bucked beneath his face, pressing his tongue deeper into the opening of her body. His strokes became faster, harder and he slid the fingers of his left hand inside her, using his thumb and mouth to bring her to a shattering climax.

Carrie screamed, jerked, and clutched at him before collapsing against the carpet in exhaustion. "Oh my God," she exhaled, running her hands over his shoulders before gripping the sides of his face. "That was..." she broke off, searching for the right adjective. She settled for an underrated, "incredible."

Ty was sliding up her body, his hard thighs splayed. He stopped inches short of her face, his throbbing shaft close to her parted lips. "Take me, Carrie. I need to feel your mouth on me."

Obligingly, Carrie's hands lifted, closing around the base of his penis. Her coral-tinted lips closed over the head and she sucked gently, rolling her tongue over the smooth skin. Her fingertips gently kneaded the skin covering his testicles and she felt his muscles bunch. Moving her head back and forth, she tortured him with her teeth, lips, and tongue, nibbling, sucking, and licking him.

Ty's hands reached back to caress her breasts, massaging the firm mounds of flesh as every muscle in his body strained for release. Perspiration coated his skin and his abdomen clenched as the first wave of release poured over him. He leaned forward, dropping his hands down on either side of her face while he willed his breathing to return to normal. "Now, that was incredible," he breathed. He pulled away from her and slid back down her body.

Carrie shifted to allow him space beside her. "And we're just getting started."

Ty sat up, pulling her up beside him. "I've poured us a glass of wine in the kitchen. Of course, it's probably warm by now."

Carrie's eyes twinkled as she got to her feet. "I like warm wine." She walked toward the kitchen, pausing to throw him a blatantly erotic glance over her shoulder. "It has so many uses."

Ty scrambled to his feet and hurried after her.

Jarod lit a cigarette and took a deep pull, drawing the nicotine into his lungs. Standing in the shadows, his face was hidden from the view of the crowd gathered inside, preparing to wish him a happy birthday. Hating being the center of attention, he opted to hide out until Jennifer forced his hand. He leaned against the wooden railing of the deck at his back and crossed his legs at the ankles, watching the throng of people just inside the glass doors.

Jennifer was dressed elegantly in a simple, red cocktail dress that showed off her slender curves and compact figure. With her long, brown hair and almond-shaped eyes, she gave any man reason to look twice. He couldn't, for the life of him, begin to understand why he was growing disinterested. He heard the doorbell ring and watched Jennifer sail across the room to answer the summons.

As the door swept open, Jarod felt his muscles tighten. Carrie stood just over the threshold, wearing a skin-tight sapphire dress that shimmered when she moved. Skimming low just over her full breasts, it hugged her body like a shiny glove and made his hands itch to take over. Standing at her side was the tall, brown-skinned man who'd become her shadow since arriving in Peking just a few short weeks ago. Jarod didn't like him. He couldn't explain his reasons behind the dislike, but there was something about him that just didn't ring true. And he knew all about lies and dishonesty. He'd perfected the art.

The glass door rolled open and Jarod straightened, pasting a welcoming smile on his face. "Hi, Babe." He extinguished the cigarette and greeted Jennifer with an enthusiastic kiss. "Have I told you lately how much I appreciate your going to all this trouble just for me?"

Jennifer snuggled in his arms. "It wasn't any trouble at all, Jarod. You know I love you. I would do anything for you."

Jarod tried not to think about how she might be put to the test in the near future. Dropping his hand to her hip in a possessive gesture, he growled low in her ear. "I guess we'll just have to see about that later tonight."

Boldly, Jennifer cupped his crotch, surprised to find it rock-hard beneath her palm. "That was fast."

He pulled her into the darkness. "I can be even faster."

She giggled against his groping hands. "We have guests waiting."

"You can tell them it took you awhile to find me." He was already unbuttoning his trousers, even though he suspected that making love to Jennifer wouldn't appease the ache between his legs. With a twirl, he whipped Jennifer around, pressing her back against the railing. Lifting up her short dress, he yanked down her panties and plunged into her without giving her time to adjust to the sudden invasion of his body.

Jennifer gasped, clutched at his shoulders and rode the wave of pleasure that rolled through her as he pounded his body into hers with unwavering intensity. She came within minutes, her head lolling back on her neck and gasping his name.

Jarod groaned low and dropped his head to her shoulder as his own climax ripped through him. He planted a kiss on her cheek and took a step back away from her, restoring his clothing to proper position. "Thanks, Sweetheart." His knuckles grazed her chin. "You really know how to wish a guy happy birthday."

Jennifer shook off the sudden uneasiness that swept through her and gave him an overly bright smile. "We should get back inside before they send out a search party."

"There's something wrong with Jennifer," Carrie whispered as Ty tipped his head down to hear her.

"Like what?"

"I'm not sure. She's not acting like herself. I'd better go talk to her."

"Go ahead. I'm going to keep an eye on Jake...or Jarod, rather."

Carrie gave him a frosty look. "I doubt he's going to do anything at his own birthday party, Ty."

He gave her a grin and pressed a kiss to her forehead. "Go talk to your friend, Caroline. I'll handle this."

Feeling dismissed, Carrie restrained herself from stomping across the room. Seconds away from Jennifer's side, she was intercepted by her mother, who, on the arm of Davis Winslow, looked the picture of elegance and grace with the exception of the frown marring her perfect features. "Hello, Mother."

Candace's hand tightened on the sleeve of Davis' wool jacket. "I am at a loss to explain the reason why you thought it appropriate to bring your lover here tonight."

"He was invited."

Candace swept a disapproving glance toward her daughter's best friend. "Well, there is no accounting for taste, I suppose. I would request that you avoid any public displays of affection. You have your future to think about."

Carrie's temples began to throb. "Mother, are you worried about Ty's lack of a college degree or the pigmentation of his skin?"

Candace's lips pinched. "I am only considering the possibility that you may become mayor."

Davis cleared his throat and intervened. "I do not think that this is the time or the place for this conversation.

Caroline, please consider your mother's wishes tonight. We shall save a place for you at dinner."

"Then you'd better save two," Carrie returned quietly.

Candace's eyes snapped back to her daughter's. "You cannot expect me to condone your illicit affair, Caroline."

"There is no illicit affair. Ty and I are both consenting adults. We are free from any romantic entanglements and we are both of sound minds. If we choose to sleep together, that is our decision."

Candace was seconds away from swooning. She fanned her face with her clutch bag and gave her husband a pleading glance.

"As I said, this is not the place or the time to discuss your...er...involvements," Davis replied with a slightly mortified glance over Carrie's shoulder. "Especially since your young man is approaching."

Candace pulled away from Davis' arm and dropped her hands to her side. She waited until Ty reached her daughter's side before she spoke. "Mr. Hamilton, it is good to see you again."

Ty inclined his dark head shortly, reading the true meaning behind the woman's words loud and clear. Deliberately, he dropped an arm around Carrie's waist. "Honey, Jennifer wants to talk to you when you get a moment."

Candace's clutch bag increased in speed as she continued to fan her face. "Davis, I think I would like some fresh air. If the two of you would excuse us...." Propriety forced her to offer the words before Candace hooked her arm through her husband's and steered him toward the front entrance of Jennifer's cottage house.

Carrie leaned against the solid wall of Ty's chest and tipped her face up to smile at him. "You enjoy pushing her buttons, don't you?"

"You can't have a conversation with your mother without pushing something, Caroline. The woman has more buttons than a switchboard." He steered her over to where Jennifer stood by herself in the corner of the living room. "Now, I'll leave the two of you alone to talk." He bent down and brushed his lips over hers, giving Jennifer a wink.

Jennifer gave her friend an envious look. "Jarod used to look at me like that."

"And you think he doesn't anymore."

"I know he doesn't. Now, he looks at you like that."

Carrie's eyes widened. "What are you saying?"

"I'm saying that my boyfriend has the hots for you." She held up one slim hand, adorned with a simple, gold pinkie ring. "Oh, don't get me wrong. I'm not blaming you. I think it's the thrill of the unknown. Jarod wants to know what it would be like to sleep with you. I guess he thinks if you can satisfy a man like Ty, well, you know."

Carrie's eyes were still rounded to horrified O's. "Jenny, I am so sorry. I didn't even notice. I mean, I didn't see. I guess I wasn't paying attention."

"With a man like Ty Hamilton in your life, it's no wonder you don't notice the Jarod Demings of this world."

Carrie admitted the truth behind her friend's words. "Well, I'm still sorry. I never meant, I mean, I hope you don't think I've done anything to encourage him."

Jennifer waved a hand in dismissal. "Don't even think about it. I just realized it tonight. He's kept his eyes on you all night long and then he left the room all of a sudden just a few minutes ago. He's either taking a cold shower or beating off in my bedroom." She gave a slight laugh and tipped back her glass of scotch. "And you want to know the funny part? He just screwed me about thirty minutes ago. Yeah, out on the deck. He was all over me. Now, I know why. He'd seen you at the door, in that dress and he got a hard-on. I guess any hole will do when you're horny."

Carrie shook her head sadly and touched Jennifer's arm. "Is there anything I can do?"

Jennifer tossed back the rest of the alcohol. "No. I'm just going to wait for Jarod to put in another appearance and then I'll talk to him. Until then, I'm going to fortify myself with scotch and water." She started toward the bar. "Want one?"

"No, thanks. Jenny," Carrie's soft voice captured her friend's attention once more, "you should probably go easy on that stuff. You know what it does to you."

Jennifer gave her a look that clearly said she didn't give a damn before continuing her journey to the bar.

"Ladies and Gentlemen, could I have your attention, please?" Jennifer was standing in her stocking feet in the center of the polished, mahogany coffee table, a drink held aloft in her hand. Her eyes were bright, the damning results of one too many glasses of the liquid she was holding out to the crowd. "Thank you so much for coming." She gave a giggle and clapped her free hand over her mouth. "Sorry, private joke. Isn't that right, darling?" She fixed her accusing gaze on Jarod's perplexed face. "I was going to make a toast to the birthday boy, but I think I'll use this time instead to ask him what he wants for his birthday. What is your wish, Jarod? If you could have anything or anyone you wanted in the world, what would it be?"

Carrie placed her glass of ginger ale down on the counter behind her. "I've got to get her down from there."

Ty's hand clasped around her wrist, halting her progress. "I don't think she'd appreciate the interruption."

"She's drunk."

"And everyone here knows that, but what they don't know, is their poster boy isn't as perfect as he claims."

"Now isn't the time for her to educate the town." She peeled his fingers away from her wrist and threaded her way through the crowd of people clustered around the coffee table.

"Oh, there she is!" Jennifer crowed with delight, sweeping her arm wide until her index finger pointed at Carrie. "There's your birthday wish, Jarod! Don't you want to take her? Well, come on, don't be a coward."

Jarod's face flushed with fury while an audible gasp reached the ears of every attendant in the room.

"Get that woman down from there!" Candace's voice whipped like a lash, fury in every syllable.

"Jennifer, please come down," Carrie held out her hand.

Jennifer twirled around, her arms held away from her sides as she pirouetted in a drunken little dance. "Oh, don't worry about me, Carrie. I can take care of myself...even without a man. You know," she stopped long enough to waggle her finger at her friend, "I don't blame you for not being interested in Jarod. He can't possibly be as good in the sack as your man." Her eyes searched the crowd for Ty's tall form. "Looking as good as he does, he would have to be good in bed. Don't you think so, Jarod? I mean, that is why you want to sleep with Carrie, isn't it? Because she looks good in that dress, right? Hell, she looks good in everything she wears, but I'm sure you know that already." Hiccuping, Jennifer began her dance once more. "My boyfriend wants to sleep with my best friend! It's like something straight out of a movie."

"Jennifer, for God's sake, get down from there," Jarod took a step toward her, reaching for her.

"Don't you touch me!" She stopped long enough to hiss at him before spinning around again. "Just keep your hands to yourself. You just slept with me but you were pretending it was her, weren't you? You wanted it to be her!" She halted abruptly, sinking to her knees atop the shining wood. "Damn you, Jarod Deming! I love you and you only want my best friend! How do you think that makes me feel?"

Accusing eyes pinned Jarod to the wall, awaiting either his adamant denial or his damning confession.

Jarod tugged at the collar of his expensive, white dress shirt. "Jenny, this is something that we should discuss in private."

"I don't want to discuss anything with you." Jennifer got back to her feet, rounding on him. "It won't do you any good, you know. Carrie will never sleep with you. She doesn't find you attractive at all. I mean, take a look at who she sleeps with. Do you really think you could measure up to that?" She leaned forward, her eyes focused just below Jarod's belt buckle. "I mean, I know how you measure yourself, but," she angled a look over her shoulder, searching for Ty's tall form above the crowd. Locating him, she flashed him a wobbly smile, "I can't imagine that you would meet Carrie's standards...which is why she's with him and you're with me. Or you were with me." Drawing in a breath that escaped on a sob, Jennifer fell to her knees once more, covering her face with her hands.

Ty parted the crowd with quiet murmurs and made his way to the table. Giving Jarod a look that said more than any words could, he scooped Jennifer up into his arms and headed toward her bedroom.

"Oh dear God," Candace whispered in horrified tones. "Someone should have stopped her."

"I think she said what she felt needed to be said," Carrie replied before following Ty down the hallway.

Chapter Five

"I cannot believe that she sleeps with him," Candace shuddered delicately while her hands busied themselves with placing the curlers in her hair in preparation for the next morning.

Davis lowered the thick novel he was reading, peering at his wife from over the edge of his bifocals. "Jennifer?"

Candace caught her husband's eye in the oval mirror. "No, of course not. I am referring to our daughter and that...that...carpenter or whatever his job is this month."

Davis returned to his book. "It's a phase."

Candace slammed the comb down on top of the boudoir table she'd had imported from England and whirled around on the cushioned make-up stool to glare at the mayor of Peking. "Our daughter is having an affair with a man that is clearly less than her equal and may very well hurt her aspirations for the future and all you can say is that it is a phase? What has gotten into you, Davis?"

"Maybe I'm jealous." He grumbled.

Candace arched an eyebrow. "Jealous? What in the world are you talking about?"

He lowered his book once more. "Never mind, Candace. Why don't you just come to bed? We can discuss this later."

The frilly white gown billowed out around Candace's slim form as she got up from the dressing table. "Sometimes, I just do not know what to think about you. You seem to suddenly have a total disregard for your daughter's political future when just a week or so ago, you were the one pushing her to run for mayor." She slipped her feet out of the lined slippers and swiped at a wrinkle in the sheet on her side of the bed.

Davis had returned his attention to the political thriller. "Whatever you say, dear."

She straightened, hands on hips. "Davis, look at me when I talk to you."

"If I did that, I would always be looking at you."

Candace never took offense; she'd perfected the art of revenge, instead. "Darling, I know that you have been under an inordinate amount of pressure as you prepare to retire, so in the interest of standing behind you, I am going to let that remark slide. However, I simply cannot overlook your lackadaisical attitude toward Caroline."

"It is not my attitude toward Caroline that concerns you as much as my attitude toward the man she is dating."

Candace slid beneath the sheets, tucking the designer sheets around her legs. "However you choose to put it, my point is still the same. You are leaving your daughter's future to chance. I would think that, as her parent, you would want to ensure that she has a future. Can you not understand what I am trying to tell you?"

Davis placed the bookmark on the page he had been trying to read for the past five minutes and closed the book. Placing it on the bedside table, he slid lower onto the bed and lifted the comforter up around his neck. "I understand perfectly, dear. I'll talk to Caroline first thing tomorrow morning and nail down her decision to run for mayor."

Only slightly mollified, Candace switched off the Victorian lamp that was more decorative than functional. "Well, at least that is a start."

Davis didn't reply as he lay there, hoping that Candace would allow him to succumb to sleep without further conversation.

Carrie sat by Jennifer's bed, one hand covering the pale, slim hand that was laying atop the thin, cotton blanket. "Ty, I can't leave her like this."

He touched her shoulder. "I know. I'm going to go get you a change of clothes. Is there anything else that you need?"

She reached for the hand that was closed around her shoulder. "Just you."

He gave her a smile that warmed her to her toes. "You've got me."

Her breath hitched in her throat. "At least for as long as it takes you to arrest Jarod or Jake, whatever in the hell his name is."

He chucked her under the chin gently. "Don't think about the future." It was how he was staying sane.

Carrie looked away. "I come from a long line of worriers, Ty. We always think about the future."

"Then I'll teach you how to live for today."

"I think you've already started your lessons."

Jennifer stirred on the bed, flinging her arm over the edge. Her head rolled on the down-filled pillow and she opened one eye. Her tongue darted out to lick her dry lips.

"Carrie, what happened?" She winced as the words reverberated through her skull.

Carrie's hand tightened around her friend's. "You had a little too much to drink."

Jennifer lifted her free hand and pressed it against her forehead. "I remember...oh God, did I really stand on top of my coffee table?"

Carrie traded glances with Ty who nodded shortly and excused himself. Carrie waited until the door closed behind him before she responded. "Do you want the truth?"

Jennifer closed her eyes. "Never mind. You just answered my question. What was I thinking?"

"You weren't thinking. It was the scotch."

"I can't blame all of that on the scotch." She clutched at her rolling stomach. "Oh, God, I think I'm going to be sick." She shoved against the blankets tangling her legs and pushed her way out of the bed to stumble to the connecting bathroom.

Carrie winced at her friend's distress, feeling helpless. As Jennifer stumbled out of the bathroom, she got to her feet and helped her back to the bed. "I'll get you a cold wash cloth and an aspirin. The best thing for you to do is to sleep the rest of this off. You're going to have a killer of a hangover when you wake up in the morning, but you'll survive." Her lips twisted. "We all do."

Jennifer clutched at Carrie's hand. "I didn't accuse you, did I? Because I don't blame you, not one bit. It's Jarod's fault. He's the one who..." her voice drifted off and her head lolled to one side. Soon, gentle snores filled the room and Carrie smiled, brushing her hand over her friend's soft, brown tresses. No matter what had happened or what had been said, they were friends and they would always be friends.

Carrie made it to the office Monday morning, but her mind wasn't on her work. Rolling her chair to the window, she watched the busy street below and wondered where Ty was, what he was doing. Then her thoughts switched to her friend. While Jennifer had seemed fine when they'd parted company late Saturday evening, there was a difference in the woman's manner. She'd been calm, pleasant, but almost distant. It unnerved her.

Jennifer had been her friend for as long as she could remember. They'd shared everything, including the chicken pox. Carrie couldn't imagine her life without her.

Her eyes riveted on the street below as her father's commanding figure exited the post office and headed toward the corner. He waited almost impatiently for the light to change so that he could cross the street. She swallowed the groan in her throat. Just as she thought; he was headed her way. Damnation.

With a push of her foot, she skidded the chair back to her desk and jabbed the intercom button. "Andrea, my father is on his way here. Would you tell him that I'm in a meeting, please? I have a lot of work to get caught up on and I just don't have the time to discuss my political aspirations with him."

Andrea's voice was laced with humor as she responded in the affirmative.

Once again, Carrie underestimated her father's abilities. A slight inclination of his head the only acknowledgement to the staff's presence, Davis Winslow sailed past the two women, his steps sure and firm as if he belonged in the office.

Carrie spun around in the chair as her office door swung open. "Dad?" Startled, she was halfway out of her seat before Davis waved her back to a sitting position.

"Keep your seat, Caroline. I came to talk to you."

She sat. "Let me guess why. You're here because Mother sent you and because you want to know if I'm going to run for mayor. Well, you can tell Mother that I'm fine and I know what I'm doing and the answer to your unspoken question is yes." She surprised herself with her sudden decision, but spoken aloud, it sounded right. She knew she had the ability to be mayor, that she could do a lot for Peking, with or without her parents' approval. She saw her father's face light up. "Yes, Dad, I am going to run for mayor and furthermore, I'm going to win. Perhaps this will make Mother happy."

"For a space," Davis concluded. "But she still doesn't like your choice of companions."

"You mean lovers."

His face colored and he tugged at the neat knot in his tie. "Well, I don't know that I would put it that way, Caroline, but the simple answer is yes. Your mother feels that you are going to limit yourself."

"Why? Because he's blue collar and I'm not? Or because we are open with the fact that we are sleeping together? Which do you think it is, Dad? Because, personally, I think it has a lot to do with the fact that, because Ty is not upper class, Mother feels that he is beneath me." She gave a wicked grin. "Well, you can tell her that he is...some of the time."

Davis was growing more uncomfortable with each passing minute. Ordinarily, he left such discussions in Candace's capable hands. He'd only come to discuss his daughter's future as the possible mayor of Peking, Georgia. He certainly had no intentions of discussing her sex life or the object of her desire. He mentally shuddered at the mere thought of continuing the conversation. "Well, those are things that should be discussed directly with your mother. I don't need to know anything about what you and your young man do."

"And what do you think of my young man, Dad? I mean, I know you have an opinion. You have for most of my life anyway."

Davis' brow furrowed as he tried to dissect whether or not he was being insulted. "I have no dislike of Mr. Hamilton."

"But you don't like him, either."

"I do not know him well enough to be able to form an opinion. Perhaps if we spent more time together, I would get to know him and..."

"Mother hasn't spent any time with him at all and yet, her opinion seems to be set in stone."

"Your mother and I don't always agree on everything, Caroline."

She refrained from snorting her disagreement. "Well, I'm sure the news that I'm running for mayor will please Mother."

Davis sat down opposite his daughter, folding one ankle across his knee and fixing her with a forceful glance usually reserved for peons who were attempting to stand in his way. "I think you should give your mother's concerns some serious consideration."

Her eyebrows lifted. "So you do agree with her, after all."

"This isn't about whether or not I agree with her. Since you have decided to run for mayor, I would think that you would want to focus all of your attention on your campaign. I know an excellent campaign manager who will serve you well and of course, I will assist you in any way possible. I don't think, however, that your young man is going to fit into the whirl and busyness of a campaign. I mean, if he's out of place in Peking now, can you imagine how he's going to feel when the campaign really gets under way?"

"I think Ty can hold his own in any situation."

Davis uncrossed his legs. "Well, I wouldn't presume to know Mr. Hamilton as well as you do, dear. I'll just leave this between you and your mother."

"And I wish Mother would just leave this between me and Ty."

Davis peered at his daughter with his keen-eyed gaze. "Do you really think your young man is the staying kind?"

Carrie swallowed and looked down at a contract lying face up on her desk. She was supposed to have it ready by the end of the week. At the rate she was going, she wasn't so sure she was going to be able to make it. "That's something that I'll discuss with Ty."

Davis nodded shortly. "Very well. I'll throw your hat into the ring. You're probably going to run unopposed, so I can't imagine that you'll have any difficulty in securing the position. The election will be more of a formality than anything." He got to his feet. "Call your mother sometime today. She really is quite distressed over this situation."

"She wouldn't have to be stressed, Dad, if she would let me handle my own affairs."

Davis cocked one eyebrow. "You're having more than one?"

Carrie laughed shortly. "No, I'm not. Ty is all I can handle right now."

"He certainly is very large. One would think twice about crossing a man like that."

"Not mother."

Davis' lips twitched, but he quickly schooled his features as he replied. "Your mother would cross the National Guard if she disapproved of them. I'll see you later, dear."

Carrie watched her father leave, wondering if she'd scored a small point in his eyes or if he was just humoring her. With Davis, it was always hard to tell. He could appear to support your actions on one hand and then do a three hundred sixty degree turn and lambast you for a poor choice. She guessed she would just have to watch out for the knives directed at her spine.

Sharon stood behind the counter at the diner, trying to appear busy as she dried the same saucer for twenty minutes. In reality, her attention was focused on the couple sequestered in the corner of her restaurant.

The tall, dark man with the long braids and killer smile had arrived first and with just a perfunctory nod, he'd made his way to the back table, obviously waiting for Carrie to arrive. He hadn't waited long when Carrie had swept through the glass doors. The bell had jangled and Sharon had looked up from the coffee she'd been pouring into old man Patterson's mug. She remembered quite clearly because she'd overflowed the cup, spilling it into the saucer and the old man had bitched about it.

Placing the saucer aside, Sharon leaned her elbows on the countertop and strained to hear snatches of the conversation.

"So you're going to run," Ty leaned back against the ladder back chair and tipped it up on two legs. "Is that really what you want?"

Carrie's eyebrows furrowed. "Of course it's what I want."

"I don't think it is."

"You've known me for a grand total of three weeks. Do you really think you know me so well you can tell what I want out of life?" She knew her voice carried a snap, but she didn't apologize. Her only concession to her bad temper was the lowering of her eyes as she awaited his response.

To her surprise, Ty stretched a hand across the table and captured her fingers. "Carrie, I'm not your enemy. I know that you want to do what is right for everyone involved."

"Jennifer is avoiding me." She quickly changed the subject.

"She doesn't know how to treat you."

"She doesn't have to treat me any differently than she normally does. It's not her fault that Jarod is attracted to me." Carrie exhaled loudly and dropped her face into her hands. "When did our friendship get so complicated?"

"Complications always come when relationships are involved. Before I came to Peking, Jennifer was happy with Jarod and he was happy with her. It was only when I came that Jarod began noticing you. That happens sometimes."

Carrie bit down hard on her lower lip. "Are you still intent on arresting him?"

He blinked. "That's my job."

"But Jennifer really does love him."

"That doesn't change the fact that he's a criminal, an escaped convict. He will be arrested."

"Don't you ever bend the rules?"

"I already have."

"When? I've been around you for these last three weeks and I haven't seen you bend one solitary rule."

"I slept with you." He lowered his deep voice to avoid the sentence carrying to straining ears.

Carrie straightened, wrapping her fingers around the handle of her spoon. "So that was against the rules."

"Always."

"Could you get fired?"

He chuckled. "No."

"If there are no consequences to breaking the rules, then, what is the purpose of the rules?"

"There are consequences, but my job isn't in jeopardy. Are you ready?" He slid out of the booth and tossed a denomination onto the tabletop to cover the coffee. Extending his hand, he helped her to her feet.

"So what are the consequences?' Carrie allowed him to help her into her short jacket.

He pressed his lips against her ear. "Trust me on this one, Ms. Winslow. This isn't something you need to know about."

She stopped dead center of the restaurant. "They could send you somewhere like Antarctica, couldn't they?"

With his hand at the small of her back, he ushered her toward the glass doors. "They could, but they won't." He lifted his hand to push against the door just as it was tugged out of his grasp. Dark eyes lifted and connected with the strained gaze of Jarod Deming.

"Mr. Hamilton, Carrie, I'm so glad I ran into you. I need to talk to you...to someone...anyone. No one will talk to me now."

Ty exchanged glances with Carrie before shaking his head. "I don't think we're the people you need to be having a conversation with right now."

Jarod's hand shot out and caught hold of the sleeve of Ty's leather jacket. "Please. It's important that I talk to someone."

"Have you considered the priest?" Carrie queried sweetly.

Jarod's gaze darkened. "You think I want to be attracted to you, Carrie? Do you think I wanted to ruin my relationship with Jennifer?"

"Let's take this conversation out into the parking lot," Ty instructed, using his body to force Jarod to back away from the door. Several steps away from the curious gazes of the diners, Ty waved a hand to instruct Jarod to continue.

"I never wanted to feel anything for you; it just happened."

"I never gave you any reason to feel anything for me, Jarod. I only liked you as a friend."

Jarod dragged his hands through hair that was already in desperate need of a comb. "Carrie, I love Jenny. I still love her. I suspect I always will. I don't know what came over me. I mean, don't get me wrong. Any man in his right man would want to...well," his gaze slid to Ty's glower and he finished hastily, "be with you, but I knew long before Jennifer found out my attraction for you, that I didn't stand a hope in hell of ever having you. You have always been way out of my league."

Carrie didn't soften. "As far as I'm concerned, you're way out of Jennifer's league, too. She deserves so much better."

He lowered his head, drawing in a deep breath. "You're right. I know that I should just walk away and leave her alone, but I can't. I love her. I can't even imagine my life another day without her." He reached out to touch Carrie, but Ty blocked his arm, giving a quick, sharp shake of his head. He dropped his hand back down to his side. "All I'm asking from you is just one conversation." He lifted his head and pinned her with a pleading glance. "Will you please talk to Jennifer?"

"And tell her what, Jarod? That I think you're an upstanding guy who deserves a second chance?" Carrie's words dripped sarcasm and disdain, reducing the man in front of her to little more than the shed skin of a rattler.

"For God's sake, I didn't cheat on her! I admitted that I was attracted to you! That was it! Plenty of men are attracted to other women, Carrie. It doesn't mean the end of their relationships. I didn't act on it!"

"Only because you knew your chances for survival were slim," she returned icily.

Ty placed a hand on Carrie's shoulder and squeezed lightly. "Carrie and I need to talk about this. We'll let you know."

A look of relief passed over Jarod's features. "Thank you. I hope that you don't think any less of me because I was attracted to your woman."

Ty's eyebrows lifted. "I can assure you that there's nothing you could do to make me think any less of you than I already do." His hand closed around Carrie's bicep and he guided her toward his car.

Carrie shook his hand off. "Are you crazy? Why on earth would you tell that snake that we would consider his preposterous notion that we would go to bat for him?"

"It was an easy way to end the conversation." Ty shrugged and opened the passenger door. "Besides, part of what he said made sense."

Carrie angled her body toward his as he slid into the driver's seat. "You're standing up for him?"

"I didn't say that."

"I guess it's really true then. Men do stick together."

"Not anymore than women do, but I'm not going to have a gender battle with you, Carrie. This isn't about men and women. It's about Jarod, or Jake, rather, and Jennifer."

Carrie flopped back hard against the seat. "Oh, what difference does it make? You're going to arrest him anyway. So it's better that Jennifer get over him now than to have to get over him a few weeks down the road."

"Maybe, but if they truly love one another," massive shoulders lifted in a shrug, "who are we to stand in their way?"

Carrie's mouth fell open. "Aren't you the same man who told me that this guy is a criminal, that he's going to jail?"

Ty adjusted the rearview mirror before slanting her a glance. "He is a criminal and he is going to jail, but he's still a man. He can still fall in love."

"But what happened to conspiracy to commit murder and all that crap?"

"What about it? The charges stand." He stuck the key in the ignition and started the engine.

"So you're not concerned about what he might do to Jennifer?"

"I don't think he would hurt her."

"What makes you so sure?"

"A man that really loves a woman isn't going to hurt her."

"What world are you living in? It happens all the time."

"When does it happen?"

Carrie never expected him to call her on it. She thought for a minute. "Men that claim to love their wives cheat on them."

The Porsche rolled out into traffic. "Then there's something lacking."

Carrie threw up her hands. "Oh, here we go. There's something lacking in the woman or in their bedroom to make them go look elsewhere. This is so typical."

"You didn't let me finish," his voice was tight.

Carrie blinked at him, an indulgent smile on her face. "Then by all means, finish. I'm here to be enlightened."

"There's something lacking inside them."

The saliva dissipated inside her mouth. "So you're saying that you would never cheat on a woman that you were with."

"Carrie, why don't you just ask me what you really want to know?"

"I thought we were talking hypothetical."

"But you want to know if I would ever cheat on you."

She didn't respond to the statement.

The Porsche slowed to a stop as he directed it toward the curb. Killing the engine, he turned to face her. "I would never intentionally hurt you."

"There's that word...intentionally. Lots of things happen unintentionally, Ty."

"True, but we control most of what happens." He leaned closer to her to see her face. "You still haven't learned to trust me yet."

"You'll be leaving soon."

He tapped one finger against the steering wheel. "That's true as well...as soon as I get what I came for."

"You didn't just come for Jarod, Jake, or whatever his name is then."

Breaking another rule, Ty shook his head. "Jake Spencer stole a large sum of money before he hauled ass out of Atlanta. We believe the money is hidden somewhere in Peking. That's what I've been waiting for. He's going to lead me to the money."

"It's evidence." She kept her eyes directed out the window, refusing to meet his gaze.

"That bothers you?"

"That you're waiting for the evidence or that it's the only thing keeping you here."

He caught her shoulders and turned her to face him. "That's not the only thing keeping me here."

Carrie shook her head sharply. "Don't. We both know why you're here. I don't need any promises. I never asked you for any and I never gave you any. We're both adults and knew from the start that this could never be more than an affair."

Ty released her, his long fingers curling around the steering wheel. "Did you want more?"

She couldn't look him in the eye and deny the question. Instead, she directed her gaze toward Mrs. Abercrombie's prized roses just over the curb. "It doesn't matter. I'm tired. Could you just take me home, please?"

He started the engine. "This conversation isn't over, Carrie."

"I never suspected that it was."

The diner was, as usual, buzzing with activity when Carrie pushed open the glass door the following morning. Sharon paused in her action of pouring coffee into one of her customer's mugs. She exchanged glances with an older man seated to her left who, in turn, angled a look over his shoulder.

"Good morning, Carrie. Would you like your usual table?" Sharon tried to sound just as courteous as always.

Carrie tilted her head to one side and surveyed the woman curiously. "Is there something wrong, Sharon?"

"Hmm? Oh, no, nothing. What on earth could possibly be wrong on such a beautiful day?"

"There goes your Oscar," muttered a low, male voice from the opposite end of the counter.

Carrie walked toward the counter and slid onto the stool directly in front of the diner's owner. "If there's something on your mind, I wouldn't mind hearing it. Maybe it would explain why half of the citizens of Peking have taken to avoiding me, even going so far as to cross the street when they see me coming." She tapped her perfectly manicured fingers on the countertop. "You know, come to think of it, it all started when my father announced that I was going to run for mayor. You don't think it has anything to do with that, do you?"

Sharon's face colored and she busied herself with making another pot of coffee, although the first pot wasn't even halfway empty. "Well, I wouldn't know anything about that."

"Sure you would. You know everything that goes on in this town, Sharon. I'm asking you for a simple answer. I think you could give me one." Carrie's voice hardened as she slipped into courtroom mode, the voice she normally reserved for recalcitrant witnesses.

"Aw, hell, she just don't want to tell you that there are some people in town who don't approve of your running for mayor when you're, well, hooked up with that guy." An older man from the rear of the diner finally appeased Carrie's curiosity.

Her eyes narrowed. "What could my social life possibly have to do with my ability to serve as mayor of Peking?"

Sharon whirled around, carafe held aloft. "He isn't as concerned about the citizens of Peking as you're supposed to be, Carrie! With his city thinking, he's liable to steer you in the wrong direction."

Carrie's face tightened. "And what makes you think that he's steering me in any direction? You don't think that I have my own thoughts? You think that just because I'm dating Ty Hamilton that I can't form my own opinion?"

"You're doing far more than just dating him," the old man corrected. "The whole town knows that you're involved with him physically."

Carrie refused to comment on that statement. Instead, she focused her attention on Sharon. "Both of my parents seem to think that I'm capable of serving as Mayor and my father, as the current mayor, should know who can handle the demands of the job, don't you think?"

Sharon squirmed beneath the direct scrutiny. "You can't blame people for their way of thinking. We're all entitled to our opinion."

"So you're including yourself in that opinion, are you?"

"That man doesn't live here. He doesn't fit in here. And furthermore, I don't think he plans on staying. So what good are you going to be to our town when he leaves?" Sharon spouted, her own ire rising. "When he first came, I saw the fire in him and knew that there was going to be trouble. I'm not denying that he's a handsome one and that you're well within your rights to have a fling with him, but when it comes to our town, well, I take that a little more seriously than you do, probably. I've lived here all my life and I'll be damned if I want to see a stranger running it!"

Carrie slid off the stood, placing her hands palm down on the counter top. "Who said anything about Ty running this town?"

"It only takes a look for you to go running after him, Carrie. We're not blind. He's going to run this town alright and none of us here has to like it."

She picked up her purse from the counter. "This reeks of my mother's influence. Have you been talking to her, Sharon?"

The woman dropped her gaze to her shorn fingernails. "Don't matter who I've been talking to. I've got my own mind."

"Yes, I suppose you do. Unfortunately for me, you don't think anyone else has theirs. Because I'm dating a strong man, you've labeled me a puppet. I don't suppose it would do any good to tell you that Ty has never once tried to convince me to do anything that I don't want to do. He's encouraged me to follow my heart. My heart told me to run for mayor. My heart told me that I could run this town and maybe even make some improvements. I can see now that I should have listened to my head." She headed toward the door, her steps slow and stilted. Reaching the glass, she stopped and turned. "Don't think this means that I'm pulling out of the race. I'm still going to run and even if you don't vote for me or support me, I'm going to win. And I'm going to work hard for this town because it's my town." She walked out into the crisp morning air, veered to her left instead of toward her office and headed home.

The walk to her house took even less time than normal. Perhaps because she wasn't interrupted by any neighbors eager for a quick conversation. In fact, she was alone in her journey toward the simple frame house she called home. She tried not to think, to feel until she was safely behind doors. Then the emotions poured over her, bathing her in the fear, the betrayal and the desire to tell the entire town to go to hell.

Falling to her knees, she pressed her back against the door and covered her face in her hands, feeling the tears flow between her fingertips. There was no doubt in her mind that the town's disapproval of her relationship with Ty had little to do with his lack of citizenship and more to do with Candace Winslow's input. Using her influence, she'd convinced the townspeople that Ty Hamilton wasn't good enough for her daughter and therefore, wasn't good enough for Peking.

Her breath hitched in her throat and she looked up at the ceiling. She wanted to scream, to defend her action and demand that they listen to her, but she knew it would do no good. Candace was too good at what she did. She'd woven a tale of the future that had convinced the citizens that any relationship she had with Ty was only going to bring devastation to Peking.

What the town didn't know was that Ty was liable to be gone long before the election came around and she would be alone again, able to serve without the entanglements of a relationship and more than likely, nursing a broken heart.

She placed a hand over her heart and bit down hard on her lower lip. When had she fallen in love with the tall, handsome CIA agent? When had she allowed herself to forget that he was only going to be in town for a short amount of time, that he was only here to do a job? She had secured the walls around her heart for a reason, but Ty had managed to circumvent the protection and she'd fallen in love. Facing tomorrow without him was unfathomable, but imminent. Damn them. Damn them all! Dropping her head to her knees, she sobbed, pouring out her feelings with tears that dampened her skirt and left her feeling spent, almost unable to function.

Ty adjusted the binoculars and shifted on the fallen leaves, holding his breath in anticipation of Jarod's next move. He'd been watching him since early morning, from the time he'd pulled out of the driveway of his rented home to now, when he'd parked the small, blue Sedan behind a rusted out old shed. His attention caught the sound of metal scraping against tin and he crawled forward for a better look.

Jarod was dragging an equally decrepit tool box across the floor of the shed, his back to the door. Squatting, he wrestled with the key attached to the box before tossing back the lid. Dropping to a sitting position, he lifted a wad of large bills and held them close to his chest, his head drooping.

With zoom-in focus, Ty snapped pictures, putting evidence in clear technicolor even while he catalogued the knowledge that his time with Carrie had just drawn to a close. He'd gotten the evidence he needed. It was now just a matter of arresting Jake Spencer and transporting him back to Atlanta. A simple matter had he not gotten involved with Peking, Georgia's only attorney.

Ty jogged up the concrete sidewalk toward Carrie's front door, his heart pounding within his chest. Arriving at her office minutes before only to discover that she'd never showed up for work had him more than worried. Combine that with the looks he'd been receiving from the towns folk and he was more than certain that Carrie had gotten a taste of something that, unlike him, she had never learned to deal with.

Reaching her front door, he pounded once on the wood before trying the doorknob. It twisted beneath his palm and he pushed the door open. "Carrie?"

She rolled to a sitting position on the sofa, having crawled to its welcoming cushions minutes before. "I'm here."

He crossed the floor in three strides, kneeling down in front of her. "What happened?" His hands cupped her face while anger curled within his chest. Did this town not know what he could do to them? What he would do to them if they continued to hurt her like this? His thumbs brushed at the tears lingering on her cheeks.

Carrie curled her hands around his wrists and closed her eyes. "It doesn't matter what happened. It's over."

"Caroline, look at me." He deliberately used her full name, hoping to get a rise out of her.

Her eyes opened. "It's just something I've got to learn to deal with."

"It's because of us."

She nodded slowly. "Everyone approved as long as I wasn't running for mayor. Now, suddenly, it's not appropriate."

"Because of who I am."

"They think you don't belong here."

"They think I don't belong with you." He corrected harshly. "You're their golden child."

Her eyes flashed. "That's not true. This isn't about our citizenship or how we live. It's about my mother and her desire to remain in control of my life at all times."

"Then maybe it's time you let her know that she's not in control." His voice was sharper than he intended.

"That's easier said than done." Her hands slid down his arms. "Sometimes, I wish I could run away and hide but since I was a child, duty was instilled in me. I have a duty to my parents, to this town...a duty I have to fulfill. I wish...." she broke off, her voice thick with renewed tears. She lifted her face to his, her lower lip trembling. "Ty, I don't know what to do."

With a low curse, he pulled her into his arms, pressing her head into the curve of his shoulder. "You have to do what you know is right, Baby. No one can decide that but you."

"It feels right when I'm with you like this, but I know that it's not going to last." She pulled away from him. "Is it? Never mind. Don't answer that." She folded her hands in her lap. "I used to think that I was strong enough to handle everything and anything that came my way. I had a plan and I was going to work that plan. Now, I'm not so sure that I can."

Ty got up to sit down beside her. "Then do what you haven't planned."

"I've been doing that for as long as you've been here."

"You can't always plan your life, Carrie."

"But I do. That's how I live my life. I schedule, organize and plan. And then everything falls into place. But then you came into my life and nothing was organized any longer. You weren't planned." She gave him a watery smile. "I know that sounds strange, but you threw my life into a tailspin."

He smiled back at her. "I hope that's a good thing."

"Not for the town, it's not."

"This isn't about the town. It's about you and me." He took a deep breath and captured her hands. "There's something I need to tell you, something I came here to tell you." He plunged in before she could interrupt. "Jake led me to the money. I'm going to arrest him this afternoon."

"Why didn't you arrest him when he found the money?"

"Because I wanted to tell you first, just in case you want to be with Jennifer when it happens."

"You gave him a chance to escape."

"He's not going anywhere. I suspect he's going to try to convince Jennifer to leave town with him."

"And suppose she does?"

"They won't leave town, Carrie. I won't allow that to happen."

Her heart quickened. "You said that he's dangerous."

"He can be."

She touched his chest. "You'll be careful?"

He kissed her. "I'm always careful. I need to go do this, but when it's over, you and I need to talk."

Trying not to appear as sad as she felt inside, she stood. "Okay. I'll head on over to Jennifer's shop. Just let me know when it's over."

"You'll know."

"How?"

"Because I think that's where Jake will be." He stood up beside her and pulled her into his arms. "I want you to promise me one thing."

"Now he wants promises," she tried to tease.

"I'm serious."

"Okay.

"Just promise me that you'll do what I tell you to do this time, just until this is over."

She read the worry in his eyes and she nodded. "I promise."

He frowned. "Maybe you should call Jennifer, have her meet you here."

"She deserves to be with Jarod when this happens, Ty. She needs to know the truth." She was heading toward the door. "I promise I will follow your orders to the letter and I'll make sure Jennifer does the same."

He reached her at the door, tugged her into a fierce hug. "I don't want anything to happen to you."

"Nothing's going to happen to me," at least until he left. That's when she would fall apart. For now, she would be strong and face the ending of this saga.

He cupped her face, dragging his lips across hers in a sizzling kiss. "I know that now isn't the time, but you know that I can't stay in Peking, not once all of this is over. There's paperwork and then the trial. It's going to take some time to get this all wrapped up in Atlanta." He placed a finger against her lips to stifle any response she was intending to make. "I want you to think about something. I don't want an answer right now. Please." He waited for her nod. "When I leave, I want you to come with me." He saw her eyes widen and wondered if that was a good thing. "I know you have a life here and that you're going to run for mayor and the truth is, I think you would make one hell of a politician, but the greedy part of me wants you with me. I don't know what you want or even if anything I'm saying right now is going to make any difference in what your decision is going to be, but," he lifted thick shoulders in a shrug, "I don't want to lose you. And, I think, if you're honest with yourself, you don't want to lose what we have. We've found something, Carrie, and this town and everyone else who disapproves be damned. Something like this doesn't come around very often. We can't let your parents or anyone else decide what's right for you or me or us." He stooped to capture her lips once more, effectively silencing her words. "Just think about it. We can talk after this is over." Catching her hand, he guided her outside. If he felt the stiffness of her body, he didn't say, but deep down inside, no matter how much he wanted her to go with him, he knew she wouldn't. Her life was here just as his was in Atlanta. Fate might have brought them together, but hell was tearing them apart. He tried to tell himself that he couldn't wait to shake off this small town, but Carrie was a part of this small town. And when he walked away, he'd be leaving a piece of himself behind.

Chapter Six

Jarod didn't know how long he'd been standing at the door to the flower shop before Jennifer finally took pity on him and let him in. What he did know was that the wind had begun to pick up and the air was growing frostier by the minute. Shivering, he ducked inside the welcoming warmth of the old building, stamping his feet.

"Damn, Jenny, you could have let me in sooner. I almost froze my balls off out there."

"Don't tempt me to shove you back out," she replied sweetly, putting several feet of distance between them. "What are you doing here, Jarod?"

"I came to talk to you."

"I don't think we have anything left to say."

"You're acting like I slept with her."

"No, I know you didn't sleep with her. You just wanted to."

He sighed heavily. "I'm not denying that I'm attracted to her, but you can't shut me out because I like how she looks."

"It's more than that and you know it. When you made love to me was it my face you saw or hers?" Jennifer pinned him with the question, a bug against a canvas backdrop.

Jarod shifted from foot to foot and raked a hand through his tousled, dark hair. "I don't know what you want to hear."

"The truth."

"I never would have followed through on the attraction." He took a step toward her, his hand held out beseechingly. "I love you too much to hurt you like that."

Jennifer shook her head firmly. "I don't believe that. You were pulling away from me in the hopes that you could convince Carrie to go to bed with you." She jammed her hand on her hips. "Deny it, Jarod. Tell me that I'm wrong. You wanted her so badly that you ached with it. That's why you snatched me out on the deck the night of your birthday party. You couldn't have Carrie, but you had to have someone. You figured that I would do just fine until you could get into her pants."

"You're putting words into my mouth, words that I've never said." Jarod didn't deny the words, though.

"Why can't you just be honest with me!"

He tossed his hands in the air. "Alright! For God's sake! You want the truth, here's the truth! Yes, I wanted to have sex with Carrie. I wanted to fuck her! But it was never that way with you! I would never have made love to her just as I've never fucked you. There's a difference. With you, it's making love. With her, it would have been just sex." He jerked around and presented his back to her, his shoulders hunched. "Do you see the way she walks? Like she owns the whole damned town just because her father is the mayor. She is proud and beautiful and looks at me like I'm little more than a blip on the big screen of life. I wanted to have her beneath me, squirming. I wanted to

106

show her that I could make her scream. I wanted to hear her cry my name, plead with me to make her come. And I know that makes me sound like the biggest bastard on the face of the earth, but I never would have followed through with any of those fantasies. Because fantasies aren't meant to be fulfilled. They're elusive dreams that may bring a smile to our lips or color to our cheeks, but they aren't meant to come true." He pivoted and walked toward her, reaching out to her. "When I came to Peking, I hadn't planned on staying long. I was only passing through. And then that very first day, I saw you, looked into those big, blue eyes and I knew that I would fall in love with you." He touched her then, his hand brushing over her long, brown hair before coming to rest on her shoulder. "And I did. I fell so hard that I can't imagine my life without you." He took a deep breath and lifted his other hand to cup her cheek. "If you want me to leave, I will, but I couldn't leave without letting you know that you are in my heart. I will always love you even if we aren't together."

Jennifer blinked at him, wavering between disgust and despair. She wanted him. She loved him, but whereas her heart was steadfast in its decision to love him, her head wasn't. "If Carrie was willing, would you sleep with her?"

His hands dropped to his sides. "You just aren't going to let that drop, are you?"

"Could you just answer the question?"

Not honestly he couldn't. How could he deny what was in his eyes? If Carrie was willing, he'd take her in an instant. He closed his eyes and gripped his hands into fists. "I don't suppose it makes any difference to you that it's not going to happen. Carrie will never offer herself to me. She's in love with that black guy."

"His name is Ty and he's much more than just a black guy as you so eloquently put it. He's a man, a real man, Jarod, one Carrie can trust. Now," she pressed her hands against his chest, pushing him back, "I want you to leave."

"You're willing to throw away our love all because I had a fantasy?"

"It's more than just a fantasy. You're obsessed with her and you're not going to stop until you have her. Of course, what you need to understand is that Ty will more than likely kill you if you even try to touch her, but I suppose that's something you're going to have to learn all on your own...without me. Now, please leave."

Before Jarod could turn around, the bell above the door jangled, capturing their eyes as they looked toward their visitor.

Ty, his hand at the small of Carrie's back, walked into the flower shop, his face unsmiling. "Carrie, why don't you and Jennifer go into the back while Jarod and I have a talk?"

"If this is the part where you defend your girlfriend's honor, then spare me," Jarod began snidely. "I didn't touch one portion of her smooth, golden skin...although, the idea does have its merits."

Ty's eyes flashed, but his face remained expressionless. "Carrie." His voice carried a warning.

Carrie caught hold of her friend's arm and began a backward trot toward the supply room, but Jennifer wrested her arm away and stood her ground. "What's going on?"

"Jenny, you need to come with me," Carrie's voice was barely above a whisper.

"I'm not going to sit in the back while my shop gets destroyed."

"Ty's not going to hurt him." At least she hoped that wasn't his plan. Although, from the look in his eyes, she couldn't guarantee the safety of a few surrounding vases.

"We're just going to talk," Ty vowed, his eyes never leaving Jarod's face.

Perhaps it was the tension in the tall man's voice or the way Carrie was moving with quick, skitterish, steps toward the back room, but whatever it was, it sent Jarod's internal antenna winging upwards. Suddenly on edge, he shot a glance toward the door and edged closer toward the exit. "I have nothing to say to you, Hamilton. In fact, I think I'll be on my way."

Ty took a step to block the door. "I'm afraid I can't let you do that."

"What is he doing?" Jennifer demanded with a low hiss.

"What he's been waiting to do since he arrived in Peking," Carrie returned glumly.

Ty's hand went to the back of his jeans and he extracted a pair of silver handcuffs. "I wish we could have done this the easy way, Spencer, but easy or not, you're under arrest."

Jarod's eyes widened, a deer caught in the headlights of a slow-moving truck. "A damned cop! You're a damned cop."

"Close. I'm an agent with the Central Intelligence Agency." He extended the handcuffs. "Are you going to slip into these or am I going to have to put them on you?"

Jarod considered his options, debating whether or not he could make it past the man who was roughly the size of a small log truck. He shot a glance over his shoulder to where Jennifer still stood, staring at him with wide eyes and open mouth. He gritted his teeth and stood his ground. "What am I being arrested for?"

Ty didn't play the game. "Put these on and if you still want to talk, we'll have plenty of time for conversation while we wait for transport to take you back to Atlanta."

Jarod lifted one hand, rubbed his stubbled jaw and shook his head. "I wish I could say that I know what this is all about, but I'm at a loss here." He gave Jennifer a pleading look. "Honey, you have to believe me when I say that I don't know what he's talking about. I'm innocent of whatever he's trying to pin on me."

"Why don't you tell her about the money and while you're at it, try telling her your real name or have you forgotten it, too?"

Jarod's eyes narrowed. "You've got some real big balls there, Hamilton, to accuse a man when you have no evidence of any wrongdoing."

"The evidence I have will be turned over to transport. I don't have anything to prove to you." Ty took a step forward, his muscles flexed, tensed, waiting for Spencer to make a wrong move.

Jarod took a step backwards. "You don't want to do this. This isn't the time or the place and I'm not going back with you to Atlanta."

"Ten to one odds say that you are." Ty's voice was cold, clipped and he dropped his left hand to his side, waving his fingers in Carrie's direction.

Taking the warning, Carrie tugged at Jennifer's arm with a firmer grip. "We really should wait back here."

Jennifer hesitated, her shocked gaze whipping between her best friend's face and the man that she loved. "I don't know what to do. Jarod, what is he talking about?"

Jarod tried to laugh it off. "Honestly, Sweetheart, this is one time I'm clueless. The guy must have mistaken me for someone else."

Ty was tired of the cat and mouse game. With a sudden movement, he stepped forward and caught Jarod around the collar, backing him against the counter. His forearm braced against the man's throat, he twisted the handcuffs with his free hand. "You can tell your sob story to the judge, asshole. For now, I'm happy that you're wearing steel bracelets."

"Jenny, please," Jarod gave her an anxious look. "I don't know what he's talking about. Maybe he'll listen to you."

Carrie was still tugging at her friend's arm, refusing to relinquish her grip.

"Ty, please, give him a chance to talk," Jennifer's eyes filled with tears as she pleaded on behalf of the man she loved.

Ty's eyes lifted and focused first on Carrie's pinched face before going to Jennifer's. "I'm sorry, but that isn't my call to make. I have a job to do."

"So that's why you're here? I mean, that's why you really came, isn't it? It wasn't because of any desire to see

Carrie; it was because of Jarod. You came to arrest him."
Jennifer peeled Carrie's fingers away from her arm and
took a step toward the counter. Big, blue eyes met her
friend's stricken gaze. "You knew, didn't you? You knew
why he was here and you didn't tell me. How could you do
this to me?"

"She couldn't tell you, Jennifer. I only told her
because she was my contract through the CIA. Don't
blame her for keeping her silence; she couldn't jeopardize
the arrest." Ty's voice slashed like a sharp knife through
expensive silk, protecting Carrie.

Jennifer held up her hands. "Oh, of course. Save
the arrest at all costs. Never mind the fact that we've been
friends for all of our lives. Forget about the fact that I am
in love with this man and that I was sleeping with him. Oh,
yes, that's not important at all." She folded her arms across
her breasts. "The least you could do is tell me what he's
being arrested for."

Ty dropped a gaze to Jarod's slumped form. "He
knows."

"I'm asking you to tell me, Ty."

Carrie tried to touch Jennifer's arm, but she pulled
away. "Conspiracy to commit murder and several other
charges, Jenny. I wanted to tell you. You have to believe
that I didn't want any of this to happen. I tried to convince
Ty that Jarod wasn't the man that he was looking for."

Jennifer fixed her with a scathing glance. "Was that
before or after you hit the sheets with him, Caroline?"
Holding her hands aloft to ward off any further
intervention, she backed around the counter and headed
toward the door. "I'm sure you'll forgive me if I don't

want to hang around and listen to any more of your pleas for forgiveness. I've had enough demands for absolution to last me a lifetime." Swinging the glass door wide, she stepped out into the crisp afternoon air.

From over the counter, Ty's eyes met Carrie's and he knew the exact moment when their relationship changed...and it wasn't for the good. She was withdrawing from him. He'd forced her hand, made her risk her best friend and she'd lost...which, in essences, meant he had lost as well. Taking his fury out on the only available target, he tugged Jake Spencer up by the scruff of his neck and directed him toward the door. "Come on, there's a jail cell with your name on it."

The park was deserted at this time of the night, as was the rest of the town. The streets had rolled up at nine and Carrie was alone as she traversed the bike path, hands in the pockets of her denim jacket, the brisk air slapping against the wetness of her cheeks.

She hitched the collar up closer around her neck and swiped the back of her hand across her face. Damn tears. How much longer could she cry before exhaustion claimed her? How long had she been walking, crying and praying that there was a solution to the problems that had taken root the day Ty Hamilton had walked into her life?

Her tennis shoe scuffed the soft dirt beneath her feet as she rounded the corner, stopping beside a wooden bench. Taking a deep, restoring breath of the night air, she focused her attention on the twinkling lights of the local grocery store, one of the only cstablishments still open at this time of the night, but soon, it would close to, Mr. Bayer going home with his wife of forty years.

Her attention concentrated on the lights and the smell of the night air, Carrie was unprepared for the shadow stepping out of the darkness.

"Carrie." The deep voice startled her, spun her around, one hand clasped over her heart.

"Ty! You scared the life out of me."

He touched her, a gentle hand on her shoulder. "I'm sorry."

"What are you doing here? I thought you would be at the police station waiting for your guys to pick up Jarod, Jake, or whoever he is."

"His name is Jake Spencer," he reminded her in a tired voice. "And they won't be able to come until morning. So he's going to be spending the night in the county jail." Ty sat down on the bench and stretched his long legs out in front of him. "We need to talk."

Carrie wasn't ready for this, wasn't ready to tell him that she couldn't go with him to Atlanta. "Now is not the time."

"You're upset with me."

"Yes, I am."

"You knew that there was a chance that Jennifer wouldn't understand."

"That doesn't make it any easier to accept. She won't talk to me."

"Have you ever had a disagreement before?"

"This goes far beyond a disagreement."

"That didn't answer my question."

"Yes, we've had a disagreement," Carrie was growing more irritated with each passing second. She shifted from foot to foot and allowed her gaze to scan the distance. "But I've never hurt her like this."

"In time she will come to understand that you were really protecting her. She could have been seriously hurt had she continued her relationship with Jake."

"But that was her choice to make."

He lifted one eyebrow. "So you would be wiling to sacrifice your friend because you didn't want to interfere?"

She fixed him with an acidic stare that was lost in the darkness. "That isn't what I said. We should have told her, given her the chance to talk to him before you slapped the handcuffs on him and hauled him away from her."

Ty stood then, rolling his shoulders forward in what appeared to Carrie to be a careless shrug. "And do you really think that he would have let her walk away from him should that have been her choice? You don't know this man, Caroline; I do. He hired someone to kill a man because that same man stood between him and ten million dollars. Do you honestly believe that he would think twice about killing a woman who knew about his true identity?" He walked toward her, took her arm in his. "I'll walk you home."

Carrie stood her ground. "That's it? Case closed? Because you think you're right, the conversation is over?"

He ground his teeth together. "It's not a matter of who's right or who's wrong. The man is a criminal. He's going back to Atlanta to stand trial. There is nothing else to discuss. I can't change circumstances...not even for you." His hand tightened around her elbow. "Now, let's go."

Carrie took a deep breath and dove into the deep waters. "I can't go with you to Atlanta."

His hand dropped away from her arm. "I knew that was going to be your answer."

"Do you want to know why I can't go?"

"I think I already know. You have a misplaced sense of duty to this town and to your parents. Not to mention you want to repair the damage to your relationship with Jennifer. I can't blame you for that, but you don't owe this town one damned thing. Not that anything I'm going to say is going to make a bit of difference." He took two steps away from her, stopped and spun around to face her. "Do you really think becoming mayor is going to make a difference in how you're treated by your parents or this town?"

Carrie's back went up. "You don't know anything about this town or me. Four weeks of sleeping with me does not make you an expert."

His eyes narrowed. "It's more than just sleeping with you, Carrie. I've gotten inside you in a way no other man ever has. Look at me." His voice commanded her attention. "Look into my eyes and tell me that you don't feel the connection."

She swallowed the lump in her throat and looked away from his compelling eyes, those eyes that read beneath the self-protective layer she'd constructed around her heart.

"You don't know me, Ty. You only know what I've let you know, but there's more, things I haven't shared

116

with you because I was never sure that we had a future." The words pierced her heart even as she spoke them. She tried to tell herself that she was doing what was best for the both of him. He had a career, one that consumed him and drove him to be the best he could be. She couldn't compete with such an intangible thing. And she had Peking to think about. Now that she'd convinced herself to run for mayor, she believed that she could make a difference and hopefully change some mental opinions about herself and the way things should be run in this town. Yes, this was for the best. The words would become her mantra, hopefully helping her to survive once the door closed behind Ty's body for the last time.

He reached out for her, catching her arms and pulling her into his embrace. "That's bullshit. Look at me, Caroline. Look into my eyes." He cupped her chin, forcing her eyes to connect with his. "Now tell me that you don't feel anything. Tell me that you don't love me."

Her breath hitched in her throat. "What difference does how I feel make? We lead very different lives. You would never be happy here and I would never be happy anywhere else. This is my home, where I belong. I don't fit in with your world and you certainly don't fit in with mine. I've watched you these last few weeks and even when we're together, I can see the eagerness in your eyes to put this town behind you. You mix with Peking like oil mixes with water and the people here would never accept you because you deliberately stand out in a crowd." She touched his cheek, enjoying the warmth of his skin beneath her palm. "You don't want to fit in because that's not who you are. You enjoy making waves, causing ripples in the calm of the waters. You would drive my mother crazy in a week and for that very reason, this town would hate you. Because, although my mother and I don't connect, this town thinks she walks on water."

His hands settled on her hips and he tugged her closer. "Carrie, I don't give a damn about what this town thinks of me or your mother for that matter. I only care about you and whether it's right or wrong, I fell in love with you." He rested his forehead against hers. "People can say that we're not right for each other, that I'll never fit into your world and you'll never fit into mine. Your mother can hate me and your father can do his best to make sure that you fit into his mold, but nothing is going to change my feelings for you." He lifted his head, meeting her gaze once more. "Tell me you don't feel the same."

The tears began flowing again. "I do feel the same, Ty. I love you, but..." a sob staunched the remainder of the words and she pulled away from him. "That changes nothing. Yes, I fell in love with you and I want to be with you, but I don't want to be in Atlanta anymore than you want to be here. I know some women can give up everything to be with the man that they love, but I have too many responsibilities here. This town needs me."

He watched her backing away from him. "You want this town to need you because you're scared of being alone, of not being needed. I can only imagine what it was like growing up with your parents, but I can tell you this. You need to forget about trying to live up to their expectations. You'll never make it. Your mother will never really approve of your life because you'll never be her. And your father, well, as long as he's married to your mother, he can't approve of you. She won't give him that option. So I guess you have to decide what is more important to you...trying to prove yourself to parents who will never appreciate you or your own happiness." He reached into the back pocket of his jeans and extracted a card. "This is where I can be reached in Atlanta. If you ever change your mind...." He let the sentence trail, giving her the opportunity to say something, anything to convince him that she would change her mind, eventually.

But Carrie only took the card and looked down at the inscription, trying to see the words in the darkness. Then, shaking her head, she turned and walked away without another word, giving him the answer he didn't want.

Chapter Seven

"Well, I have to hand it to you, Hamilton, you got your man," Dave Berringer slapped Ty on the back as if the two men were the best of friends. "I'll have to admit that I had my doubts...especially when I didn't hear from you except for the one time that I called you. I thought for sure that you were going to fall through on this one. I guess you proved me wrong." Giving him a toothy grin, he sauntered toward the paneled refrigerator and extracted a long-neck bottle of beer. "Want a cold one?"

"No, thanks." Ty cast an eye toward the clock on the wall, biding his time until he could make his escape. "I'm heading home in a few minutes."

"Oh, well, some of the guys wanted to go out for a few brews to celebrate this one. This looks real good on our record, let me tell you. Sure you don't want to join us?"

Ty stood, stretched and nodded. "I'm sure. It's been a long month."

"Well, get plenty of rest then because the big boys have another assignment for you starting Monday."

"I'm not available," Ty walked toward the door.

Dave hurried after him. "Wh-what do you mean you're not available?"

Ty paused. "What part didn't you understand?"

Anger flashed in the director's eyes, but he willed himself to remain calm. "Why aren't you available? This is an important job. Some rich bitch has been kidnapped and they need a good man to get her ass out of trouble. Heard she's a real looker, too," he nudged the taller man with an 'if you know what I mean,' elbow and grinned. "Who knows? If you play your cards right you could probably get lucky."

If only Berringer knew just how lucky he'd gotten in Peking. Lucky enough to lose his heart and unlucky enough to lose Carrie. He gave the man a bitter smile and twisted the doorknob. "No, thanks. I'm not interested."

Dave followed him into the hallway, their steps muted beneath the pile carpeting. "You don't seem to understand, Hamilton. This isn't an assignment that you can turn down. The top brass want you. End of discussion."

Ty angled a smile over his shoulder coupled with a shrug. "So tell them to fire me. I'm not interested in another assignment right now. I'll call them when I'm ready to work again." He dug his keys out of his pocket and headed toward the exit.

"Cocky son-of-a-bitch," Dave muttered, glaring at the agent's retreating figure. He could only hope that this would be the last straw and that the agency would finally can the arrogant bastard. He stomped back to his office, knowing that his hopes would not come to fruition. To the CIA, Ty Hamilton was their golden child and he was barely hanging on by his toenails. Some men were just born with the luck of the Irish.

The chilly temperatures hadn't stopped the citizens of Peking from gathering in the town square to witness the induction ceremony of their new mayor. On a wooden dais, Carrie stood beside her father with her hand raised and a smile on her face. To the average viewer, she was compose, self-assured, and happy. Inwardly, a deep pain had taken root over the last two months that time was failing to help.

A strong gust of wind lifted the edge of Carrie's long, black skirt and swirled it around her shapely legs. Calmly, she repeated the words of promise to the town and in her father's eyes, she climbed up another notch on his ladder of self-worthiness.

"Ladies and Gentlemen, the new mayor of Peking, Georgia, the Honorable Caroline S. Winslow!" Davis' loud voice boomed without need of a microphone. His face wreathed in smiles, he wrapped his arm around his daughter's waist and guided her toward the front of the dais.

Amid shouts and cheers of congratulations, Carrie looked out on her constituents and wondered, not for the first time since Ty had left, just what in the hell she was doing. She had no doubt that she was capable of performing her duties as the mayor of Peking, but she had serious doubts as to whether this was what she should be doing.

Over the last two months, she'd attempted to repair the damage to her relationship with Jennifer to no avail. Her former friend wasn't returning her calls and avoided her on the street, even going so far as to open her shop later in the day so that Carrie was safely inside her office by the time Jennifer arrived to work.

"Wave at the crowd, dear," Candace Winslow whispered to her daughter from just behind her. A proper smile plastered to her face, she appeared the perfect example of a proud mother even while her eyes searched for flaws in her daughter's attire, her posture and her response to the townspeople's applause.

Carrie lifted a hand in obedience, her wave lacking in enthusiasm.

"Speech, speech!" The shouts were deafening and Carrie felt a crisp piece of paper make its way into her hand. She looked over her shoulder and her mother was nodding slightly, directing her gaze toward the paper. With a sigh, Carrie made her way to the microphone.

Clearing her throat, she captured the attention of the crowd. "Thank you." Unfolding the note, she scanned her mother's neatly written words before she lifted her gaze. "I'd like to take this opportunity to thank the individuals who worked tirelessly on my campaign, creating the flyers, getting the word out and helping me to achieve the victory over my opponent even though," she slanted a smile at the portly butcher who was waving at her in cheerful acceptance of his defeat, "I believe Stan would have made an excellent mayor. Thank you for conceding so graciously."

The man's face flushed and he ducked his head, taking an inordinate amount of interest in his shoes. He mumbled something that sounded like "you're welcome" but could have passed for, "how thick would you like your steaks?"

Carrie continued to smile as she addressed the audience once more. "I know that you're all probably expecting a speech about how I'm going to change this town and make things better." There were murmurs of agreement. "Well, I'm not going to tell you that." The murmurs ceased. "Because I can't do anything that you don't want me to do and without your help, there will be no changes. If you want things to happen in Peking, then, you're going to have to work with me. Together, we can create a town that will make us proud and entice visitors to want to take a look at us."

Davis cleared his throat loudly and stepped forward. "Okay, everyone, we have refreshments waiting in the bowling alley." He heard his wife's audible wince just over his shoulder and spared her a cursory frown. He was well aware of Candace's disapproval at his choice of the bowling alley, but he'd wanted a place where everyone would feel welcome. Never mind that his own wife didn't feel welcome there. To Davis, that was the least of his concerns. Besides, Candace was never really happy anywhere.

As the crowd began to dissipate and head toward the open doors of the bowling alley, Davis hooked a hand around his daughter's upper arm and steered her toward the edge of the platform. "I thought we'd discussed this crazy idea you had about inviting tourists to our town."

Carrie glanced down at her father's hand. "We did, but I don't think it's such a crazy idea. And neither do most of the people here. We need the income, Dad."

"Not so much that we want strangers coming here to dirty our town."

She pried his fingers away from her flesh. "They're not going to dirty our town. I don't know what movies you've been watching, but plenty of towns have tourists and they manage to survive. So will we. And we'll survive with a better economy and more jobs for our citizens. I'm going to drag this town into the twenty-first century even if it takes every bit of strength that I have."

Davis' brows beetled together. "So you plan on fighting me at every opportunity then?"

Carrie took a step back and surveyed her father with a curious look. "Fight you? Dad, you're not the mayor any longer. You don't have any decision to make here."

His face turned a mottled red. "I helped you get elected."

"You strutted around town telling anyone who would listen how proud you were of me when you and I both know that it isn't the pride as much as it was the fact that you wanted a Winslow to remain in control. And you thought, with my election, that you could still remain in power. Unfortunately, I have to correct you on that. I have no intention of being your puppet. I was elected and I'm going to serve as the mayor...without interference from my family."

"Caroline," Candace voiced her reproof in a stern tone of voice, "do not speak to your father in that manner. He has spent an extraordinary amount of time insuring that you were elected as mayor. He gave of his time, energy and influence to secure your position. You should be grateful."

"And I suppose that my education, experience as an attorney and standing in the community had nothing to do with my being elected as mayor?"

"Your standing in the community is directly linked to your name." Candace smoothed the a-line skirt she wore into proper place and hooked her elegant bag over her shoulder. "Now is not the time to continue this discussion. Your father and I will talk to you further after this...gathering of sorts." With slow, measured steps, she descended the platform, head held high, back stiff. "Come alone, Davis."

Carrie watched her parents walk toward the bowling alley and she felt the tears prick the backs of her eyes. Why had she thought things would be different? Why had she expected that her parents would suddenly sit up and take notice of her own ability when graduation from law school at the top of her class hadn't achieved that goal? Swiping her hand across her eyes, she drew in a deep breath. Well, they might have won the points today, but the war wasn't over. She was the mayor of Peking and she'd be damned if she'd back down from them now. She had a job to do and she was going to do it no matter what it took.

"Surprising news out of the small town of Peking tonight," the Atlanta-based anchorwoman intoned to the viewing audience. "Just days after the town's newest mayor was elected with almost ninety percent of the town's votes, the former mayor has challenged the victory and is pushing for a re-election."

"But that's not really the surprising part, Shannon," the co-anchor inserted with a professional smile toward his co-worker. "The former mayor, none other than the current mayor's father, wants to write himself in as another candidate. Amazingly, this had split the town in half, creating quite amount of friction. This is unheard of and we'll certainly keep a watchful eye on this small town."

Ty clicked the off button on the remote and sat back on the sofa, his arms folded. He could only imagine what Carrie was going through now. He closed his eyes, his desire to call her warring with his decision to leave their future in her hands. Soon desire won out and he lifted the cordless phone just as his doorbell pealed.

Muttering a curse, he tossed the phone aside and got to his feet, heading for the door. Switching the outside light on, he swung the heavy, oak door wide and stared. "Carrie?" He couldn't believe she was standing on his doorstep, her big, brown eyes huge in her pale face, her lower lip trembling.

"I know that I shouldn't have come. I should have called first." Carrie didn't know why she was there or maybe she did, but she wasn't sure she wanted to analyze her decision. She only knew that she had to see him, needed to see him.

He reached out and took her hand, pulling her inside. "It's okay." He pushed the door shut and faced her, his hands closing around her shoulders. "Are you alright?"

"Yes. No. I--do you know?"

"It was on the news." He helped her out of her coat and hung it on the doorknob. Then, taking her arm, he led her into the living room.

Carrie didn't take the time to notice the furnishings of the condo. Instead, she turned to face him, her heart hammering in her chest. "I know that I have no right to be here. I'm the one who made the decision to end our relationship and I should have severed the ties without looking back, but I..."

Ty placed a finger over her lips, silencing the words. "Carrie, let me hold you."

Her shoulders relaxed and she walked into his arms, resting her head against his chest, allowing him to absorb the worries of the past few days, the stress of her father's attack and sudden betrayal. It felt natural to let the fear and anxiety slip from her shoulders to Ty's.

His strong arms closed around her, sheltering her, protecting her, and he felt his world right itself. He pressed a kiss against her silky, brown hair and breathed in the scent of her shampoo and his heart restarted. With her in his arms, his life resumed. "God, I've missed you."

"I've missed you, too. When all this started, I wanted to call you, but I kept hoping this would blow over, that Dad would eventually call it off. But it's gotten worse and there's no one in town that I can talk to. Jennifer hasn't spoken to me at all and..." she broke off, catching herself before the words segued into sobs. She closed her eyes and remembered the scent of his skin, the warmth of his flesh. Her hands slid up the hard wall of his chest and she pressed herself closer to him, needing to feel the imprint of his body upon hers.

Ty knew the exact moment her needs changed, when she no longer needed a comforter, but a lover. His hands began a slow, leisurely pace over her spine before sliding down to her bottom. He cupped her soft flesh, lifting her against his growing erection. Without words, he tipped her head back and lowered his lips to hers, drinking in the softness of her lips, the heat of her mouth. "I've missed your taste," he whispered before gliding his lips over her temples, her cheeks and back to her mouth.

"Ty, make love to me." She didn't embellish on the request, knowing instinctively that he would understand her needs.

Needing no further instruction, Ty swept one arm beneath the bend in her knees and lifted her against his chest. In a few short strides, he was in his bedroom. He lowered her to the mattress and slowly began unbuttoning her silk blouse. "I've thought about touching you like this again. I've dreamed about it." He dropped a kiss to her bare shoulder.

Carrie tipped her head back and leaned back on her hands, giving him full access to her bare skin. She felt the catch on her bra give way and moved her arms to slide the lacy material out of her way. "I've dreamed about you. I've remembered this, the feel of your hands moving across my body, holding me." She tugged his head back down to her face and fused her lips to his, taking the initiative. Her tongue plowed against his, tasting his welcome.

With short, furious movements, Ty removed her skirt and rolled her panty hose down the slender length of her legs. His hands moved back up her thighs, skimming the lace of her panties before diving beneath the waistband to find her hot, moist center. She bucked beneath the intrusion of his fingers, opening herself to his quest and he groaned low in his throat, pressing tiny, heated kisses against her neck.

Her body burning, need clawing its way up her spine, Carrie shoved against his shoulders, dislodging him, tearing the shirt from his body. Eager to feel his skin against hers, she unzipped his jeans and shoved them down his muscled thighs, brushing her knuckles over the thick bulge beneath his form-fitting briefs.

Sliding down his body, she pressed kisses along the wall of his abdomen before traveling lower to touch the warm material stretched tightly over his erection. Her lips created damp patches and her teeth scraped him through the cotton. Then, with a sudden flick of her wrists, she freed him, rubbing her cheek alongside the hot length of him. She purred low in her throat and turned her head to taste him.

Ty's breath hissed out of his lungs and he caught her beneath her arms and hauled her back up onto the mattress. "Not this time, baby."

Carrie laughed and crawled up toward the pillows. On her hands and knees, she tossed him a saucy look over her shoulder. "I guess you have something else in mind."

Up on his knees, Ty caught her hips and pulled her closer to his throbbing shaft. "I have a lot more in mind." He heard the swift intake of her breath as he slid his thick penis into her moist cleft. His fingers bit into her soft flesh as his body began to pump.

Carrie's hands fisted in the pillow and she arched her spine, forcing him deeper into her body, pushing him to push her over the edge. She felt his hands moving around her hips, his fingers delving between her legs to find her pulsing nub. She moaned low in her throat and gasped his name, pleading with him.

DARK KISSES

"That's it, baby. You're almost there," Ty crooned in a husky voice, his fingers pressing against her clit while his hips ground into hers.

Carrie felt the first waves of her release crest and she lifted her legs off the mattress, a low scream building in her throat. "Oh God, I'm...Oh, God..."

"It's okay. Let it go. Let it go." He gritted his teeth, the tension building in his muscles, sweat beading on his chest and stomach. Just as Carrie screamed his name, his own climax tore through him and he groaned her name as his seed spilled into her.

Carrie collapsed against the stack of pillows, her breathing labored. "Did I mention that I missed you?"

He chuckled as he rolled to his side, tucking her against his stomach. "I believe that came up."

Carrie lifted her hand and touched his cheek over her shoulder. "I've missed this, too."

"So have I." His hand tightened around her waist. "I love you, Carrie."

She closed her eyes, a thickness settling into her throat. "I love you, too."

"Will you stay?"

"I have to finish what I started in Peking."

"Then I'll go back with you. We'll finish together." He lifted her hair and pressed a kiss against her neck.

"And then what?"

"We'll work something out. If you want to stay in Peking, we'll compromise."

She rolled over, settling herself closely against his lean body. "What are we talking about?"

He smiled into her eyes. "Isn't it obvious?"

"Maybe to you."

The smile faded. "Marry me."

Her hands cupped his face. "Yes."

He kissed her, his lips hard, firm. "Life with me isn't going to be easy."

"And what makes you so sure that life with me is going to be such a cakewalk?"

He smiled against her lips. "I'll take any kind of walk as long as it's with you."

"You do have a way with words."

"That's not all I have a way with." He took her hand and placed it over his renewed erection.

"You've got ways I haven't seen?" She smiled while her hand began a slow stroke that stoked his blood.

He pulled her close against his chest and slid his hand over her buttocks. His fingers parted the smooth skin and slid into the narrow crevice, finding the warm stickiness between her thighs. Drawing the dampness over the valley, he located the small, tight opening that had never known a man's touch. He felt her body stiffen and he soothed her with encouraging words and gentle fingers. "Just relax, baby. I'm not going to hurt you."

Carrie bit into his shoulder as his index finger slid into the small, tight opening, creating a new friction. His other hand dropped back between her thighs, moving through the dampness to massage her clit once more. It was a matter of seconds before the lights exploded and her body responded to the movement of his fingers.

Ty lowered a kiss to her lips and grinned at her. "And that was just the beginning. We've got all night."

"Just all night?" She whispered. "I thought we had the rest of our lives."

He pressed her head to his shoulder. "Amazing. The one time that you're right and I'm wrong."

She laughed against the musky scent of his skin. "I can see I'm going to have to work this cockiness out of you."

"While you're doing that, why don't I work a cock into you?" He flipped her over to her back and guided himself between her thighs.

She opened her body to accept his willingly. "I can see that it really is going to be a long night. Good thing for you that I didn't have any other plans."

"Good thing for both of us."

Chapter Eight

Silence reigned inside the confines of the Porsche as it ate up the miles toward Peking. Carrie sat with her hands folded in her lap, her ankles crossed. Occasionally, she would allow her gaze to drift from the window to Ty's profile, the handsome features creating an ache in the hollow of her stomach. Her love for him threatened to consume her, overwhelm her, but then, he would turn his head, flash her a smile and a wink and she relaxed.

Ty stretched his hand across the console and captured her hand, threading his fingers through hers. He didn't speak, just offered her support and encouragement in a way that no words could ever equal. He was there for her, would always be there for her. He brought her fingers to his lips and kissed the tips before lowering their combined hands to his thigh.

The speedometer shot past seventy, slowly climbing toward eighty just as the city limit sign came into view. Ty heard Carrie's anxiety even though she didn't make a sound. His fingers tightened around hers and he deliberately slowed to a crawl. "Do you want to stop?"

She wanted to do much more than stop. She wanted to turn, run and never show her face in the town again. But she had a job to do, parents to face and a friend to confront. She would do those things even if it killed her. And it very well might. "Yes, I want to stop, but don't. I need to get this over with."

"I'm right here beside you."

"I know. Otherwise, I wouldn't be doing this."

Even at a crawl, the Porsche crossed the city limit much too soon and rounded the corner leading into the center of town. At just after five in the evening, Peking was still abuzz with activity, working mothers on their way to daycare while fathers hurried off to the local bar to exchange anecdotes about the day only to face the fury of their wives later that evening.

Grizzled heads lifted with the growling of the Porsche's engine and Sharon dropped her dishtowel and hurried to the window of her diner. Cupping her hands around the glass, she peered into the rapidly diminishing sunlight. "Well, I'll be damned. It's Carrie and she's brought reinforcements."

"Oh, Davis isn't going to like this," one man bemoaned, although his eyes were alit with excitement at the possibility of a confrontation between the town's former mayor and current mayor. He was sure it was going to be the likes this town had never seen, which was precisely why he hurried to the pay phone in the back of the diner to call his wife. She would never forgive him if he didn't notify her of this choice morsel of news.

Sharon divested herself of her apron and grabbed her jacket. "Harvey, keep an eye on things, will you?" She called to the cook. "I've got something to take care of." The glass door whipped shut behind her and she hurried across the street, her worn tennis shoes slapping against the concrete as she beat a hasty path to the beauty salon.

The scene was set for another showdown at the OK Corral, only this wouldn't be a war of guns. But the crowd gathered in the center of town was just as eager to see the final confrontation between father and daughter. Folks had taken seats on the grass while others had procured lawn chairs from the backs of station wagons and pickup trucks. Country music was blaring loudly from several portable CD players and chilled cans of beer were visible on the freshly cut grass.

Candace stalked toward the center of the square, looking regal in a wine-colored pant suit that accentuated her slim figure and enhanced her brand-new bob which the town's only cosmetologist had just put the finishing touches on when Sharon had burst through the doors of the salon to inform her that Caroline had arrived back in town. Her hands covered in leather gloves, which matched the leather jacket that graced her slender shoulders, Candace was the picture of wealth, prosperity and class. She'd dressed to intimidate and was prepared to face her daughter with her ammunition barrel full.

Davis Winslow fell into step beside his wife, a frown marring his lined face. "You should let me do the talking."

"I would hope that you are not thinking that I am going to stand idly by while Caroline destroys our reputation as well as everything we have worked so hard to achieve. This town is as much my responsibility as it is yours."

"She is still our daughter."

"She has turned her back on her values, her beliefs, everything we have taught her, Davis. It is time for her to move on."

Davis sighed. He'd never wanted this fight. And now, he just wanted it over. He would have conceded long before now if Candace hadn't insisted that he not back down. Deep inside, close to his heart, a part of him ached for what he was about to lose...his only daughter. He saw her from a distance, standing beside the tall, black man that she'd chosen over her family, her friends, her career. And he hated Ty Hamilton with every fiber of his being. The man didn't deserve his daughter, not when he and his wife had spent the last thirty-three years of their life building Caroline into the woman that she was now, the same woman that was now turning her back on her family.

Carrie squared her shoulders, straightened her spine and prepared to face her parents. She'd been hoping to brave the confrontation in a less public place but the summons had come from her mother, insisting they meet in the town square so as to provide the proper witnesses. After all, her father was challenging her ability to lead this town. One wouldn't want rumors to get started.

She ran her hands down her knee-length navy, blue skirt and wished she'd worn something that bolstered her courage more. As her father approached, she could see the light of battle in his eyes and prepared herself for the worst. "Hello, Dad. Mother."

"Let's not waste time with preambles, Caroline. I see you brought Hamilton back with you. Moral support?" Davis chuckled at his own attempt at humor then he raised a hand to silence her retort. "Listen, I have been thinking and there is simply no need for this rivalry to continue. I...." He grunted as a bony elbow dug into his side. He clamped his lips tightly together to keep from roaring at his wife, but it didn't matter. Candace was already speaking.

"Caroline, dear, what your father is trying to say is that we have done everything to provide you with the greatest opportunities and to have you throw our efforts back in our faces like this is, well, the only way I can describe it is devastating. We have sacrificed to provide you with the money and means to achieve far more than you have. Your father groomed you for this position and now, to see that you want to turn Peking into a common tourist attraction, to invite unruly strangers into our midst when we have done everything within our power to keep out the miscreants of the world...." She broke off long enough to dab her eyes with a scented handkerchief, an effective tool used to garner sympathy. One of her oldest and closest friends approached her, placed a hand on her shoulder and glared at Carrie.

Score a point for Mother, Carrie thought wryly. She took a deep breath and plunged in. "I left yesterday because I was tired of fighting. I certainly didn't come back to fight now. I know that you and Dad have done a lot for me because you've never once let me forget it. You have reminded me daily of how much I owe you. You did not want a child, Mother; you wanted a miniscule version of yourself, a Barbie doll that you could groom to be a replica of Candace Winslow. That's why you're so angry right now...because I don't fit the mold." Before Candace could gain her second wind, Carrie continued. "But that doesn't matter now. I'm done. I'm through fighting with you. I'm through trying to please you. I know that I should probably stay and see this through to the end. After all, I did win the election fair and square and I know that I could do the job to which I've been elected, but it's not worth my sanity. Nothing here is, which is precisely why I'm resigning." She felt Ty's hand tighten around her waist. He was surprised. Just as her parents were and the entire town. Everyone was staring at her as if she'd started speaking a foreign language. Score a point for her.

Davis took a step forward, his eyes blinking rapidly. "You're giving up the job?"

"That's right, Dad. You win. You can have your office back, complete with the framed photographs of the presidents and the box of imported cigars left in the top desk drawer. You know," she tapped her chin with a polished nail, "you aren't the only one who's been thinking about this, but I'm sure we've been thinking about two entirely different things. You've been trying to figure out a way to get me out of your office and I've been thinking about why you wanted me out so desperately. I don't think it has a thing to do with the idea of tourism. I think it's because of your own sense of identity. It took you all of three days to realize that you are known as the mayor of Peking. That's all you have. When it was gone, you couldn't take it." She shook her head, sending a lock of soft, brown hair tumbling across her forehead. "And I never thought I'd say this, but I feel sorry for you. To the outward appearance, you seem to have everything, but inside, you have nothing. You can't honestly stand there and say that you are desperately in love with your wife because I know differently."

"Our marriage is not up for discussion, Caroline," the words came out on a hiss as Candace approached her daughter. "Do you really think that what you have found with this man is going to last? You do not have the makings of a marriage; you are in lust, not love. It will fade and then you will find yourself living with a man you do not even know." Even as Candace spoke, the words drove a stake through her heart, describing her own union with a perfection that had her eyes glittering with malevolence at her only child.

"Just as your marriage is not up for discussion, neither is my relationship with Ty. You will never understand how or why we love one another, but I am long past needing your approval. I came back here to resign and since that's done, I'm going home now to pack. I'll be putting my house up for sale since I won't be returning. Good-bye, Mother, Dad."

"You're really leaving?" The soft words came from behind Carrie and she spun around to face the owner.

"Jennifer. I didn't think you were ever going to speak to me again."

"Me, either, but I...don't want you to leave."

Carrie placed a hand on Ty's arm and gave him a smile before walking toward her friend. Reaching her, she enfolded her in a hug. "There's nothing left for me here, Jenny. I thought I could make a difference as the mayor, but I'm just as much a puppet now as I ever was. The only way that I can wiggle out from under my parents' thumbs is to leave, start over. I can do that with Ty." She pulled back and met Jenny's watery gaze. "About what happened..."

Jenny silenced her by squeezing her arms and shaking her head. "No, don't. I never should have blamed you. It was my own fault. I was just blind to what was really behind Jarod's mood swings and when I finally knew, I had to strike out, to blame someone." She cast a glance toward Ty's tall form. "You really love him, don't you?"

"Yes, I do. He..." she lowered her gaze and smiled. "He asked me to marry me."

Jennifer tugged her closer for another hug. "And you said yes."

"I said yes."

"I'm so happy for you."

"Will you stay here?"

Jennifer scuffed her shoe against the concrete. "I'm not sure. I have my shop, but," she lifted her shoulders in a shrug, "I'm not so sure that I want to remain here without you."

"You could always come to Atlanta."

"I'll keep that in mind. Don't forget about me." Jennifer's voice was laced with sadness.

"I could never forget you, Jenny. You are, and always will be, my best friend."

"And the offer will always be open," Ty had approached them with silent steps. Hooking an arm around Carrie's waist, he drew her close to his side. "Whatever you need, whenever you need it, give us a call. We'll help in any way that we can."

Jennifer surprised herself by standing on tiptoe and wrapping her arms around Ty's neck. "Thank you."

He patted her back and pressed a kiss against the top of her head. "You're welcome." He dropped his gaze toward Carrie's upturned face. "Sweetheart, we'd better get going."

Carrie slipped her hand into his and allowed him to lead the way through the crowd.

"Caroline, if you leave now, you are on your own from here on in. We will not be here to bail you out should you find that you have made the wrong choice." Candace's threat carried little weight and Carrie only shook her head as she headed toward the Porsche parked at the curb.

Ty helped her into the car and waited until she was buckled in before speaking. "I'll be right back."

Carrie caught his hand. "Where are you going?"

"There's just one thing that I have to do." He squeezed her fingers before pulling his hand away and closing the door. His long strides ate up the distance back toward the town square where Candace and Davis stood watching. He slowed to a stop and spared the couple a cold glance. "I don't know if either of you realize what you are losing, but Carrie is much more than just your daughter. She has heart and she loves with this amazing love that still surprises me. She really cares for people and she wants to change things for the better. That's why I'm glad she's in my life. She's changed me, for the better. She accepts me, as I am, which is more than I can say for this entire town. And despite the way you've treated her, belittled her and reduced her to tears, she has loved you unconditionally. And you're letting her walk out of your life knowing that she is the only person that loves you that way." He directed his glittering, hazel eyes toward Candace. "You think you know your daughter, Mrs. Winslow, but you don't truly know her heart. Because if you did, you would know how much this is hurting her. Instead, you're writing her off as easily as you do a charitable contribution. And you," the gaze swung toward Davis' open-mouthed gaze, "Mr. Winslow, are the weakest man I've ever met. You are standing here watching your daughter put you behind her simply because your wife has told you that's the way it should be. I've never met a more spineless excuse for a man in my entire life. If I were you, I'd put that woman," he pointed toward Candace, "out of my life and make room for my daughter. She's the only one who truly loves you."

"How dare you!" Candace spat, her eyes flashing with fury.

Ty held up one hand. "Please spare me your righteous indignation, Mrs. Winslow. I don't have time to listen to your disparaging comments about my lack of breeding, the color of my skin or what you consider your daughter's lack of judgment in choosing to love me. Right now, Carrie needs me and since I'm the only one she has that really, truly loves her, I think I'll go be with her."

He walked away, shutting out Candace's sputtering words of rage and affront.

The lights of the town winked in the rearview mirror as Ty slowed to a stop alongside the road. Killing the engine, he switched on the dome light and reached for Carrie, pulling her across the console and into his lap. Tucking her head against his shoulder he let her cry, absorbing the pain of the past two hours. "I'm so sorry, Baby. I wish things could have ended differently."

Carrie's hands fisted in the collar of his shirt. "I knew it wasn't going to be easy, but at least it's over." She lifted her tear-streaked face. "It's behind me now, in the past and that's where I'm going to leave it." She pressed her palms against his face. "Thank you for being there."

"Where else would I be?"

"I can't believe I walked away."

"Carrie, maybe that's something you should think about a while longer." He began hesitantly.

"What do you mean?"

"They're the only family that you have."

"I thought I had you."

He smiled, covering her hands with his. "You do. You'll always have me, but they're your parents. They gave you life, raised you. I know they're not perfect, but..."

"Maybe in time, but for now, we need a break, a chance to breathe without one another, to see how it feels. At least I do." She tucked her head in the crook of his neck, breathing in the warm scent of his skin. "What did you say to them when you went back?"

He wasn't about to open that can of worms. In time, maybe, but for now, he settled for a simple, "I only said what I felt needed to be said. We can talk about it later. For now, let's go home."

Carrie started to crawl back across to her seat, but Ty's hands held her fast. She tipped her face up to his. "I thought you wanted to go home."

"I do...eventually." He cupped her chin and brought her lips down to his.

Author Bio

Rachel is a published author in contemporary, fantasy, and paranormal romance with small vibrant presses. She works full time as a paralegal and also an editor for vintage romance.

See other works by this talented author at

www.Venuspress.com

Rachel Carrington

DARK KISSES

Rachel Carrington

Printed in the United States
48181LVS00001B/139